# Excerpts from Follow The Money

### *From "The Drop"*
… Clint closed his eyes and pursed his lips, wondering if God wanted him to be the older brother, why he didn't go ahead and make him the older brother? …

### *From "The Investment"*
… That's what women that looked like her did.  They never earned the money themselves; they stole it with a marriage certificate and a promise of amazing sex for the rest of your life.  You paid for it one way or another …

### *From "Sammy's Night Out"*
… The dude with the gun was jerking his head back and forth, spinning around and trying to look everywhere at once.  Sammy wondered if he'd ever done this before, stuck up a place, 'cause he didn't look too sure of himself …

### *From "A Loaded Gun"*
… Five seconds, that's all it took for Calvin to pop the lock.  Fifteen more and he had it started, some Amy Grant crap coming out of the speakers.  Junior sat there with his mouth open watching Calvin do his thing when he should have been watching for the owners coming out of the restaurant …

### *From "Everybody's Got A Magic Number"*
… He twisted at his waist, still stretching and looking like that curly-headed queer that sold the Oldies workout tapes his ex-wife always bought.  She only used them a couple times, Dwayne said once, so her ass was still the size of Montana …

### _From "Have Fun Tonight"_

… The girl EMT gasped when she saw it, her eyes widening like she was in sixth grade seeing one for the first time, like they'd snuck in the girl's bathroom during library and he pulled it out just for her …


### _From "Sweating Brother Bill"_

… Now this preacher, Brother Bill, was up there in his preacher's robe, getting himself all worked up talking about lambs and daughters and patience and lust and sin, and it was getting Ruth and Agnes all worked up watching him sweat, picturing him in tight jeans and an unbuttoned shirt, gyrating to some loud bass beat that was so deep it shook the clasp on your wonder bra …


### _From "Toe Thumb"_

… As soon as she opened the front door, Frankie heard Fayrene neighing like a horse in heat.  When Frankie got back to the bedroom, she saw Fayrene with her legs in the air, Harold between them giving it to her hard with nothing on but black socks …


### _From "For The Road"_

… Wally shrugged to himself and got out, pulling up his pants cause he never had a belt that was the right size.  They were always too tight or too loose, never fit like the belts on the models in the JC Penny ads.  Of course, JC Penny didn't have models with a gut and cowboy boots …


### _From "Channel Ten"_

… Talking about how he was raising money for America's youth, how they were coming up short on how much it was costing to build _Savior Land USA_, and if you could find it in your loving heart, send in twenty or forty or, God bless you a hundred or two, and they'd be able to construct the main attraction, the Screaming Tower of Babylon …

# Follow THE Money

A collection of
interconnected
short stories.

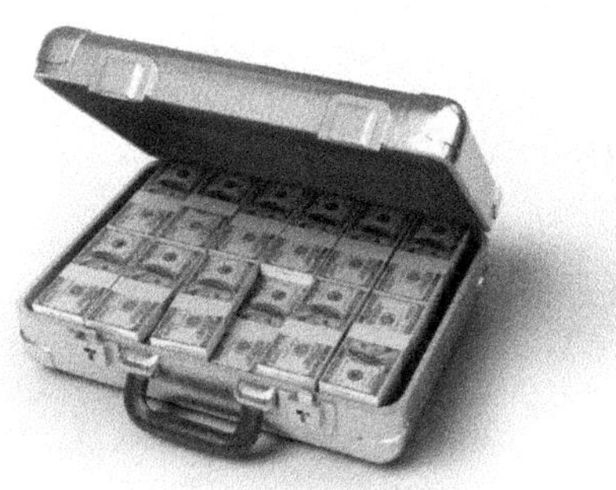

# Ross Cavins

This book is a work of fiction, mostly. Names, characters, places and incidents are either products of the author's ubiquitous imagination or are used fictitiously. Any resemblance to actual events or locales or persons, living or dead, is entirely coincidental, except in those passages where you may see a likeness of people you know or, in the small chance, no matter how remote, suspect that it indeed may be you. If so, you know who you are, and now you can go around telling people you're in a book. If you are annoyed by this and attempt to sue me, I will feign ignorance and eventually, someone with a wooden bat will come visit you in the middle of the night and persuade you to drop the suit.

I dedicate this book
to my entire family.

Without their unwavering support (money),
it would not have happened.

Oh yeah, I guess I should mention
something about their unconditional love too.

*Special Thanks*
*to*


**Jeff Brown** and **Ric Thomas**
for most of my initial feedback and encouragement.


**Robert McClure**
for his editing expertise and frank suggestions,
even when it meant extensive rewriting.


**Julie Anthes**
for her insightful opinions and editing help and for
fawning over me when I needed it most.


**Swill Magazine**
for originally publishing "Sammy's Night Out."
SwillMagazine.com


**Hiss Quarterly**
for originally publishing "Have Fun Tonight."
TheHissQuarterly.net


**Carmen**
My amazingly intelligent, hottie wife.
You weren't in my life when I wrote the book,
but you are now and I'm a better man for it.
Thanks for the re-editing advice.
I want to have your babies.

"Writing is like prostitution. First you do it for love, and then
for a few close friends, and then for money."


*Moliere*

Follow THE Money
Follow The

# About the Book

It began with a single short story:  "Sammy's Night Out."  The initial response from friends was overwhelming; I was flattered.  One even said, "You're one funny dude."

With this kind of encouragement, I set out to write more short stories about the adventures of Sammy.  I got as far as the ideas; the culmination of stories just seemed too flat.

Then I discovered it wasn't Sammy that was so great, it was his character.  He's the prototype of today's Redneck and everyone has a real Sammy in their life.  So I thought, "Why not write stories with the same types of characters instead?"

I mean, *write what you know*, right?

"The Drop" came next.  And then the motif of money presented itself one morning before coffee had restored linear thinking.  I wrote "The Investment" and then came up with a story around Sammy and his night out; and the rest, as they say, is history.

If you're a fan of Elmore Leonard or Carl Hiaasen, you'll find that my work is heavily influenced by them:  the characters, the situations they're caught in, the humor that surrounds them.  And why not? They're veritable masters of the written word and if you've never read their books, you're missing out on some amazing journeys.

I truly hope you enjoy reading my short story collection as much as I enjoyed writing it.

# Table of Contents

"The want of money is the root of all evil."

*Samuel Butler*

# #1

# The Drop

THE GIRL WAS in the back room, asleep.  Clint and Waylon sat in the kitchen, drinking beers at the little table Clint picked up at Goodwill last year for five bucks.

"Where we doin' it?" Waylon asked.

"I don't know yet."  Clint scraped at the label from his Budweiser.  He heard somewhere it gave you luck if you got it all the way off without tearing it.  There had to be a trick to it.  He'd figure it out, pull it off in one piece.

"I thought you had it all planned out."

"I do, just not all the little details."

"Little details?  Where we do it is like one of the big details, ain't it?"  Waylon turned up his beer, taking three big swigs one right after another.

"Hey!" came a muffled voice from the back room.

Clint took a drink from his beer.  He looked at the label, half off now and not a tear yet, thinking that was a good sign.

"Hey!"  The girl screamed again through the closed door.  Waylon glanced at his younger brother, waiting for him to do something.  Clint sat there in his chair, leaning back studying the label on his beer bottle like it was a winning lottery ticket and he just had to scratch the right boxes to win.  The girl yelled again for somebody to come there.

"You gonna see what she wants?" Waylon finally said, fidgeting in his chair like a two year old that's got to go to the bathroom.  Do number one.

Clint shrugged, keeping his eyes on his beer bottle.  It was sweating pretty good now, making it easier to peel the label off but also making it just as easy to tear.  "You go see what she wants."

* * *

WAYLON HESITATED, rocking back and forth, looking down at his beer.  He finally slipped on his pantyhose mask just past his nose and left the kitchen, beer in hand.  The floor of the trailer creaked in the hallway where it was rotting through.  Clint said they had to replace part of the sub floor, whatever that was.  But that wouldn't matter any more, they were getting a real house when this was over.

Waylon opened the door to the room just as the girl yelled one more time.

"Whatcha want," he said, looking at her sitting on the bed, rubbing her left wrist, the one that was handcuffed to a chain wrapped around the bed frame.

"I gotta pee."  She looked up at Waylon with her ocean-blue eyes, the ones that Waylon said to Clint made him uncomfortable like she could read his mind.

"Lemme go ask my brother."

"You have to check with him on everything?  You go take a shit, you ask him if you can wipe your ass?"

Waylon's mouth dropped open.  "No, I … I gotta check with him … he's got the key."  He turned back toward the kitchen and yelled, "She's gotta pee."

"So let her pee," Clint yelled back.  "What you asking me for?"

Waylon turned to the girl.  She had an eyebrow raised and held her wrist out, the one with the handcuffs him and Clint bought at the Army Surplus downtown last week when they got the idea to do this.

"I gotta get the keys," he said.  He came back a minute later with his beer in one hand and the keys in the other.

The first thing she did when he unlocked her was reach for his beer. Waylon's reaction was to jerk it back from her but he was too slow, her surprising him like that.  She turned the bottle up while he looked at her, still unsure what he should do.

"You're too young to drink," he said finally.

"I am, am I?" she said as she took another swig, never breaking eye contact like they were in a staring contest.

"Yeah, yeah you are."  Waylon didn't reach to get it back though.

"Well, you know what I think?"  She turned the bottle up, finished it and handed it back to him.  "I think I'm too young to be held captive against my will, what do you think?"

"I think you better get your smart little ass in the bathroom, is what I think," Clint said as he appeared in the doorway.  Waylon and the girl turned to see him with his pantyhose stretched all the way over his head, a black Dale Earnhardt cap on top with a light halo surrounding a red number "three" embroidered in the center.  He held his beer in his hand, the label missing except for a little corner hanging raggedy on the side.

The girl handed Waylon his empty bottle and shot Clint a look of defiance as she squeezed by.  He didn't move out of the doorway when she passed.

"Why you let her talk to you like that?" Clint said to Waylon when the bathroom door closed.

"Like what?"

"Like she the one in charge, not you."  Clint lifted his pantyhose and turned his beer up.

"Huh?"

"Whaddya mean, huh?  She's just a kid, man, and you let her treat you like *you're* the kid."

"She don't talk like no kid."

"Are you kidding me?" Clint said smiling.  "She's worse than Uncle Eddie when he gets to drinking with his construction buddies.  And lemme tell you, that man knows how to cuss."

"And she don't act like no kid."

"You can say that again."

"And she definitely don't *look* like no kid."

"Yeah, you got that right."  Clint's smile grew big and he made round motions in front of his chest.  Clint almost whispered, "Don't seem right to put titties that big on a kid, does it?"

Waylon snickered and lowered his voice too.  "How big you think them things are?"

"I don't know, but they bigger than Aunt Louise's, ain't they?"

Waylon thought about it, then said, "Yeah, I think so but you ever see Aunt Louise in a bathing suit?"

"Yeah, I know."  Clint wrinkled his nose.  "They's flabby with stretch marks but she still puts 'em out there for everyone to see.  Bet the kid's don't look like that.  Bet they's a lot nicer."

The sound of the toilet flushing shut them both up but they still sported childish grins when the girl came out of the bathroom. She wore a t-shirt that said Hilfiger and a pair of jeans so tight Waylon had to force himself not to look at her rear when she walked by.

* * *

BACK IN THE ROOM, the girl sat on the bed and stared at the brothers. They looked back at her. No one spoke. Finally, to Clint, she said, "See something you like?"

Clint smiled and shook his head, thinking they better get this over with fast before he started wanting to do things with this girl he didn't really want to do. Would be something to teach this little rich girl a lesson, though. Show her she can't just shoot off her mouth any time, snap her fingers and get everything she wants. Show her what a real man's like.

She looked at Waylon, forcing him to look straight into her eyes, and said, "How about you, big boy, you see anything you like? Huh?" That last part, she wiggled her shoulders gently like Mae West in one of them old black and white movies where people talked a lot.

The part of Waylon not covered in nylon turned pink.

She laughed and said, "You know, that pantyhose on your face is worthless."

"Whaddya mean?" Clint said. "Pantyhose is a good disguise."

The girl rolled her eyes. "Not when you leave family pictures up." She nodded with her head toward the dresser. On it was a picture of Clint and Waylon, Clint holding a twelve pound bass and Waylon with the net they used to get it in the boat.

"Shit, Waylon. You were supposed to get all that stuff outta here."

"Yeah, well," Waylon said. "You ain't supposed to use our names either."

"Shit. Well, this is all fucked now." Clint yanked the hose off his head and put the cap back on, saying, "Come on, Waylon." He motioned with his head to leave the room and go back to the kitchen. "If you good,"—looking at the girl now—"we'll let you hang out for a while without being handcuffed. But don't be causin' no problems."

The girl looked like she wanted to say something smart, but held her tongue till they closed the door. "What if I'm not good?" she said through the door while Clint and Waylon walked back to the kitchen. "Hey! What am I supposed to do to entertain myself?"

"There's a TV in there," Clint yelled back. "Turn it on, catch up on your soaps."

"I don't want to watch TV."

"Well now, that's tough shit, ain't it?" Clint pulled two beers from the fridge and threw one to Waylon.

Waylon pulled his pantyhose off and said, "So where we gonna do this thing?"

Clint looked at him. "I don't know yet. Have I had any time to think about it since the last time you asked?"

"Hey!" The girl opened the door and peered down the hallway at them.

"Jesus Christ!" Clint said, his voice getting loud. "What is it now?" Looking down the hallway at her.

"I'm hungry." Her head was peeking out from behind the door, her sandy blonde hair pulled back in a ponytail now, hanging down pointing at the floor.

Clint took a deep breath, then said, "Whaddya want?"

She opened the door a little more, then a little more so that she was standing there in full view. She yelled, "Steak and fries."

"How about a baloney sandwich or some cereal?"

"Oooh, I want cereal," Waylon said as he walked over and opened a cupboard.  He pulled out a box of Peanut Butter Crunch and Clint took it from him and put it back.

"You eat too much of that damn stuff.  You'll rot out your teeth," he said.

"How about pizza?" the girl countered.

Clint looked at Waylon, saying can-you-believe-this-girl with his expression, then sat down and popped the top on his beer by placing the bottle against the edge of the table with the cap biting into the wood, and ramming his fist down on it real quick.  He didn't care it was a screw top; he liked to open them that way.

"What?" she said.  "All that money you're going to make off me and you can't spring for a stupid pizza?"  She stood there with her hands planted on her hips, looking at both of them.

"I wouldn't mind a pizza either," Waylon said to Clint, sitting down beside him.

Clint breathed out and shook his head with his eyes closed.  "I'll bet you want one of them veggie pizzas, bunch of mushrooms and green peppers and shit like that," he said to the girl, who'd taken a few steps out into the hallway while his eyes were shut.

"Hell no.  I want pepperoni or sausage or maybe an all-meat pizza.  Maybe some garlic breadsticks and chicken wings."  She walked into the kitchen, pulled out a chair and sat down beside Waylon, across from Clint.

Clint almost asked her what the hell she thought she was doing, but wasn't in the mood to argue about it.  He got up and went to the fridge, pulled the Mister Pizza magnet off, and went over to the phone.  He called in a large meat lovers and an order of wings while he watched the girl drink Waylon's beer, belch like a fat man, and take another swig.  The whole time, Waylon just sat there and let her do it, looking at her look at Clint while she chugged.

Clint opened the fridge when he returned the magnet, grabbed another Bud, and walked over to the table, handing it to Waylon as he said, "Here, I got you your *own*." He watched the girl drink Waylon's other beer, then sat down across from her again. "Pizza'll be here in twenty."

Waylon, his face scrunched, said to the girl, "What kinda name's Eustice?" Actually pronouncing it right: *YOU-stis*.

"I know, tell me about it." She rolled her eyes. "That's the same question I've had every day of my life. Soon as I turn eighteen, I'm changing it. That'll be my birthday present to myself. A hundred and three days from now."

Clint looked at her. "You know how many days it is exactly? Just like that?"

Eustice nodded. "Yep, even down to the hour. Wouldn't you if you were named Eustice?"

Clint thought about it, then said, "Yeah, I guess you got a point there."

"Damn skippy I do. I asked my parents once a long time ago about my name. My mom said it was my great-grandma's name, Nana Eustice. Said she was a strong woman with a strong name." The girl took another swig. "She was supposed to be one of them that helped pave the way for women to vote."

"Really?" Waylon said.

"Something like that. Well, I told her, 'Keep a picture of her in the living room, don't name *me* after her.' Then my mom says she thinks it's a pretty name so I tell her she should change *her* fuckin' name to Eustice."

She paused. "And then she smacked me up side the head with a Bible. Told me I needed to learn some manners or she'd learn them for me."

Clint and Waylon looked at each other.

Eustice continued, "I said to the bitch, 'You ever hear of a model or actress or a cheerleader named Eustice?'" The girl shook her head. "Nope, maybe a truck driver or a miner. Not anybody pretty though, I'll bet you.

"I asked my mom once if she'd take me to get my name changed and she said she'd rather cut off her left leg. Said she won't ever let me do it and if I did it when I got old enough, she'd disown me right then and there."

They sat at the table drinking their Budweisers, looking at each other, looking out the window and looking at the clock on the microwave.

"So how much you guys going to ask for?" Eustice asked.

"What's it matter to you?" Clint replied, leaning back and propping his feet on the corner of the table.

She shrugged and threw her hands up. "I was just asking. No need to have a cow over it."

Clint looked at her, thinking how he barely even said anything, but this girl was acting like he made a big fuss.

"I mean, how much research have you done?" she said.

"Whaddya mean?"

"I was just wondering if you had any idea how much my daddy was worth? So you'd know how much to ask for. I mean, if he's worth like a hundred million and you ask for ten thousand, you're losing out big time. You know what I'm saying?"

Clint nodded, his brain spinning while he thought of a reply.

Waylon was looking at him now, his eyebrows knitted together like he was expecting an answer too.

"Well?" the girl said when Clint didn't answer her. "You ever do any research? How much are you going to ask for?"

Clint decided to fish a little. "How much *you* think we should ask for? See if you're close." *Maybe ask for double what she said.*

Eustice looked at him with narrowed eyes. "You don't know, do you? You don't know how much to ask for. You don't have a fucking clue." She smiled like she just came in and caught him looking at a nudie magazine with his zipper half down.

"Sure I do, I was just seein' what you thought."

"Well, I think you're full of shit. That's what I think. You're wanting me to tell you a good number to ask for."

Clint was quiet for a minute before saying, "Alright, how much should we ask for?" Then added, "Since you know so damn much."

Eustice licked her lips, looked Clint right in the face, and said, "Two, maybe three million. But the more you ask for, the longer it'll take him to get it. He's got it tied up in stocks and stuff like that. He'll have to sell them first. I saw a statement about a year ago from his broker that said he had five million in stocks."

"Why not ask for all five?" Waylon asked, sitting up straight in his chair now.

"Cause if we ask for it all," Eustice said while she rolled her eyes, "he might want to get the police involved. But not for a couple million. He'd probably keep that quiet."

"Yeah, stupid," Clint said. "That's why I do the thinkin'. Wait."—looking at Eustice—"*We? We* ask? When did *we* start to include *you? We* means me and my brother. You're the one *we's* holdin' to get the money."

Eustice took a big gulp of Budweiser and belched. "Not any more. I want half." She looked at him again with those eyes that Clint swore were older than her driver's license said.

"Half? Are you fuckin' crazy? Half?"

"I'm the key to all this working, right?"

"You're fuckin' nuts, wantin' half our damn money. *You're* the fuckin' hostage. You don't get no money. You get to go back home."

"I don't want to go back; I hate it there.  I want enough money I can go away and never come back.  Ever."

"Little girl, you ain't gettin' no half our money and that's that."  Clint sat his beer bottle on the table and leaned forward like he was meaning business.

Eustice took a breath and let it out.  Drank a swallow and made one of those *ahhh* sounds, then said, "I'm not a little girl.  I'll be legal in a hundred and three days."—looking at Waylon while pouting her lips out—"I'm practically legal now and like I said,"—looking back at Clint—"I'm the key to this whole thing.  I could get up right now and leave, do this all by myself and you wouldn't get anything."

Clint stuck his chin out now.  "Try and leave, see what happens."  He gave her a serious look, like Clint Eastwood gave all them guys in his movies.  His mama said he was named after the actor 'cause she always thought he was what a real man should be like.  Clint could do a pretty decent impersonation of him, too; turn his voice gravelly and tell somebody to make his day, punk.  Had all his movies on DVD, even the old westerns and the one with the boxing chick.

Eustice laughed and said, "You wouldn't hurt a fly.  I don't even think you have a gun.  I could tell when you took me outside the mall last night it was just your hand in your coat pocket.  I could see it in your eyes you were faking it.  I just came along to see what everything was about."

"That's bullshit, we didn't give you no choice 'bout comin'."

Eustice laughed again.  "I've been a brown belt for two years; was going for my black belt next month.  I could have taken both of you out inside of twenty seconds."

Clint's face slackened and his eyebrows raised slightly.

"Still could if I wanted to.  *What?*  You look surprised.  You not do any research at all on this?"

"Yeah, right," Clint said, calling her bluff.  Waylon visibly relaxed as Clint said, "Well, if that's so, why you let us take you, huh?"

"I thought you were going to try and have sex with me."  She looked at Waylon as she said it. His eyes widened and his ears turned red.

The doorbell rang.

Clint got up and started toward the door, then looked back as Eustice raised both her hands, palms out, as if saying she wasn't going to do anything.  Clint opened the door and gave the delivery boy a twenty, told him to keep the change.

Clint had never tipped the guy no more'n a dollar or two no matter how many pizzas they ordered, even for the Daytona 500 party they had last year when they ordered ten large pizzas.  Tipped the same kid two dollars then, saying to the guys, "What?  All he did was carry'em from his car; how hard is that?"

Clint dropped the pizza and wings on the table and went to the fridge. "Get me another," he heard the girl say, right before she turned hers up and finished it.

He threw a Bud to her and she caught it in one hand, right side up, not even grinning afterwards, like it was nothing to her.  Unscrewed the cap, fixed it between her thumb and middle finger, and flicked her wrist while snapping her fingers.  The bottle cap flew across the room in a pretty arc like a Michael Jordan three-pointer and landed square in the trash can in the corner.  Didn't even touch the walls, went straight in.

Waylon laughed and clapped his hands, looking from her to Clint and back to her again.  Clint gave him a hard stare but Waylon wasn't paying any attention, still clapping like that damn retarded kid did down the road every time he saw a red car.  Somehow, back a few generations, they were related but Clint didn't tell anybody.  Explained about Waylon though.

Clint grabbed some paper plates and napkins and threw them on the table beside the pizza, saying to dig in before it got cold.  Eustice kept up with the guys, eating as much as Waylon and Clint, drinking with them beer for beer.

"Alright," she said finally.  "I'll settle for a third.  I guess that's fair, even though I could find somebody else and split it fifty-fifty."  She shrugged.  "You're already here."

*Here?*  Clint wasn't believing this girl.  *Here* was his damn trailer, bought and paid for.  *They* the ones that got *her,* not the other way around.  She was acting like she interviewed them for kidnapper positions, checked references and after a long debate, finally chose them over thirty other applicants.

*But still, it would be a pretty easy job if she was helping instead of fighting them.  Not to mention the fact she had seen their faces.*

Clint said, "We ask for three million, we each get a mil.  I think we can make that work, whaddya think, Waylon?"  He looked over at his brother who was grinning with hot wing sauce on the sides of his mouth, been there all meal 'cause they ate the wings first.

"Great!" Eustice said, standing up and pushing her chair away from the table, grinning like a girl who'd finally found the dress she wanted to wear to the prom after looking through a hundred catalogs since she was twelve. "I'll be back in a minute and we'll make the call."

"We don't know where he is right now," Clint said.

"I do."  She winked as she turned.  "That's why you got me."  She walked off down the hall, and turned into the bathroom.  Clint could have sworn he heard her humming under her breath.

"Whaddya think?" Clint said to Waylon when she'd closed the door.

"'Bout what?"

"'Bout her gettin' a third."

Waylon shrugged.  "I don't know."

"Well," Clint continued, "we ain't gonna give it to her."

"We ain't?"  Waylon's eyes widened.

"Hell no we ain't."  Clint kept his voice low and they heard the toilet flushing.  "Okay, here she comes."

But the door never opened.  Instead, they heard the shower turn on.

"What the hell?  She takin' a bath?" Clint said.

"Sounds like it."  Waylon said.

"Well, anyway," Clint continued, shaking his head, "we ain't givin' her no money at all, much less a million bucks.  She's crazy she thinks she's gonna get a million dollars from us when we done all the work.  That's us payin' her a half-a mil each; you realize that?"

Waylon thought about it and said, "I never saw it that way."  His face was scrunched up like a kid passing gas and he still had the sauce on the sides of his mouth.

Clint handed him a clean napkin and made a motion like he was wiping his mouth but Waylon just stared at him.  He did it again, made the motion, and Waylon still didn't get it.

"You got sauce on you," Clint finally said.

"Yeah?  Where?"

Clint closed his eyes and pursed his lips, wondering if God wanted him to be the older brother, why he didn't go ahead and make him the older brother?  Wasn't that the way it was supposed to work?  "On the side of your mouth," he finally said, reopening his eyes.

"Which side?"

"Both," he said through clenched teeth.

Waylon wiped his mouth and asked, "So where we gonna do it?"

*God, just like a damn kid wantin' to know if we's there yet so he could take a piss.*  Clint held himself in check, saying flatly, "I don't know yet."

Then added, "Somewhere deserted where we can see if he's gonna try and double-cross us."

"Deserted, like an old abandoned house?"

"Uh … no … not exactly. Just somewhere there ain't gonna be no people, some place we know our way around and he don't."

"How about the church?"

"No, not at the church either. Give it a rest, okay? I'll think of something if you quit interruptin' my thoughts with your yakkin'."

Waylon looked at the used napkin in his hand, turned it over a few times, then said, "Sorry."

Clint brought his left hand up and rubbed his temples. "No, Waylon, *I'm* sorry." He was remembering the last thing their mama said before she died of lung cancer from smoking three packs of Salem Lights a day. Pulled him to her at the hospice and held his ear close to her mouth 'cause the cancer'd spread to her voice box when she switched from cigarettes to dip and she couldn't talk real loud.

First, she coughed so hard that something came up and stuck to his ear and he pulled away, only to be yanked back down by her strong old hands, and then she told him, "Clint, you take good care of your brother. When I go, all you'll have is each other and he needs you. He'll always need you, dumber than a box of rocks he is. God gave you all the brains in the family and with that comes—" and then she coughed up another glob of something that hit him square in the cheek, sticking in the beard he had at the time. Took a full five minutes to scrub that gunk out in the bathroom and by the time he returned to her bedside, she was gone from this world. He was pretty sure her last word was going to be "responsibility," only it ended up being "comes." But in his memory, he went ahead and gave her credit for "responsibility."

Waylon looked up 'cause it wasn't often Clint said he was sorry.  Clint continued, "Waylon, I know you mean well but just lemme think about it a minute and I'll come up with something, okay?"  Waylon nodded without making a sound.

They sat there, drinking beer and staring at the empty pizza box, listening to the shower run until Clint yelled out, "Hey!  You gonna use all the damn hot water?  Hey, you hear me in there?"

The water cut off and Eustice yelled back, "What?  Are you talking to me?"

But by then, Clint was looking at Waylon, smiling and saying, "That's it!  Down at the old rock quarry where we used to get drunk and go swimmin'!  That's where we do it."  Nodding and talking to himself, repeating that last part over and over as he leaned back in his chair and turned his beer up.  "Yep."  He tried to belch as loud as Eustice but didn't get close.  "Down at the old rock quarry.  Why didn't I think of that sooner?"

The bathroom door opened and out came the girl with a towel wrapped around her tanned little body, the material barely holding in her breasts.  It stopped just below her special place and Clint imagined if she stretched her arms up they'd see a piece of heaven.  She walked into the kitchen, Waylon and Clint watching open-mouthed the whole way, and reached for her beer on the table.  The towel opened up, exposing her left side up over her hips and Waylon dropped his bottle to the floor, making the beer in it shoot up over his head.  The bottle bounced once, then fell over and began glugging out.

Waylon jumped up and bent over to get the bottle while Eustice laughed at him. The whole time Clint was watching her towel open up even more and hoping it'd fall off while she was laughing, thinking she definitely weren't no little girl.  Then, while Waylon was grabbing the rest of the napkins off the table to sop the beer up with, Clint came to his senses and told her to "go put yer damn clothes back on."

Eustice, still laughing, her chest heaving with each breath, looked at him and said, "Does this towel bother you? You want it back?" She brought her hand up to the top and locked a finger underneath it like she was going to rip it off.

Clint, not missing a beat, said, "As a matter of fact, I do." Keeping his eyes locked with hers, holding his hand out, calling her bluff again. Waylon sat straight up in his chair, staring at her, eyes bugging out and mouth in the shape of an O.

Eustice held the gaze with Clint for a few moments before finally saying, "You wish." Then turned and strutted back down the hallway and into the bathroom, Clint and Waylon watching her work her hips the whole way.

Waylon said in a whisper, "How big you think her melons are?"

"I don't know," Clint said back in the same whisper. "But we almost found out, didn't we?" Both of them grinning till their cheeks hurt.

When Eustice came back out of the bathroom, she was fully dressed with her wet hair up in a towel turban. She sat back down in her chair and asked for another beer. Clint wondered why she didn't get it when she was up.

"Why you wantin' to do this?" Waylon said to her.

"Take my parents for a couple million? Easy, I hate them and everything they stand for."

"Hate 'em? But they's—"

"I know who they are, *please* don't remind me. Every day I wake up, I know who they are. I can't leave the house without it slapping me in the face. Believe me when I tell you that as far as parents go, they're the worst you could ever possibly have. All my mom ever thinks about is what piece of jewelry she's buying next and all my dad does is plan his stupid amusement park."

"But—"

"But nothing.  Can you imagine having to be perfect every second of the day because if you're not, it reflects on them?  That's something they've reminded me of every single day of my life.  Do you have any idea what kind of pressure that is on a girl?  Do you?"

While Eustice was ranting and Waylon was saying "but," Clint had gotten up and pulled another beer out of the fridge and given it to her.  She unscrewed the top now and chugged it.

"I want to run away," she said through the silence.  "I don't want to ever have to see them again and I want the whole world to know they suck as parents.  I want to hurt them the way they hurt me for the last seventeen years."

Clint and Waylon were at a loss, them not having any idea what that felt like, to hate your mama and daddy.  Both theirs were gone now and they loved them as much as possible, always had.

"I'm going to Vegas," she said.  "I'm going to be a famous stripper because it's everything my parents would hate."

"A stripper?" Clint said.  "But you're too young to be a stripper.  You gotta be at least eighteen to do that."

Eustice smiled.  "That's why God created fake ID's.  I know someone who can make me one in ten minutes and I can have any name I want.  No more stupid *Eustice*."  She paused, then said, "Well, let's call daddy.  I can't wait to make him pay."  She stood, grabbed the phone and began dialing.

Clint thought "What the hell?" because he wasn't ready yet, didn't know what he was going to say exactly.  He wanted to write it all down so he'd get it right and not screw it up.  But now the girl was dialing her daddy's number and thrusting the phone at him.  He took it and gave her a mean look but she acted like she didn't see it.

"Hello," said a voice on the other end of the line just as Clint put it to his ear.  Clint cleared his throat and tried to disguise his voice as best he could, doing his Clint Eastwood impression, gravelly and cool like Dirty Harry.

"Is this the Reverend Billy C. Reid?" he growled.

"This is him … who is this and how did you get my private line?"

Clint smiled.  "Your daughter gave it to me."

"My daughter?  You're with her?  Well you tell her that this staying out all night isn't very funny.  Her mother and I have been worried sick.  She's grounded when she gets home, and we've decided to take away her car for a whole week.  We'll see how she likes that."  Clint noticed that the Reverend's voice sounded a lot different than it did on TV.

"She's not coming home," Clint said raspy-like.  "Not until you pay us three million big ones."

"What?"

"I think you heard me.  Eustice is our hostage and we'll kill her unless you agree to pay us three million bucks by tomorrow at noon."

"Wha … wha … I … I don't have that much money."

"It's two o'clock, maybe you ought to start sellin' some of your stocks and bonds.  Cause that three million's gotta come from somewhere and it's gotta be in our hands by noon tomorrow or you'll get your daughter back piece by piece."

"I … I … I want to speak to Eustice.  Put my Eustice on the phone."

Clint handed the phone over to the girl, her smiling 'cause he'd used the piece-by-piece line from some movie he'd seen, pulled it right out of thin air the moment he said it.

"Daddy!  Daddy!"  The girl went from calm and smiling right to hysterically screaming into the phone, playing her part like a pro, like she'd been planning this a long time.  "Oh *please*, Daddy!"  Even throwing in some crying and sniffling sounds.  "Please, daddy, pay them or they said they'd … do things to me and take pictures and put them on the internet.  Oh God, Daddy!"  She thrust the phone back at Clint.

"Eustice!  Oh Eustice!" the Reverend was saying.

"That's enough, Reverend.  You heard the girl.  Tomorrow, by noon.  I'll call you on this line.  And Reverend?  No police and come alone or I take pictures."  He hung up.

Eustice immediately screamed for joy and jumped over to him trapping him in a bear hug, pushing her big titties all over him, then kissing him on the cheek.  Next she attacked Waylon who stood there as rigid as a mannequin, his eyes wide and unblinking.

"That was great!" she finally said, backing off and shaking with excitement.  "You know what my dad's biggest fear is?  A scandal, that's what.  And the nightmare he's always had was me showing up in one of those Girls Gone Wild videos and being identified as his daughter.  That scares him worse than me being a hostage, because a scandal can take down everything he's ever built.  No more ministry, no more TV show, no more international crusades.  And you know what that means?" she asked, putting her hands on her hips again, then bringing her hands out and counting off.  "No more mansions, no more limos, no more followers, no more money."  Eustice looked triumphant, the happiest since they'd picked her up.

Eustice took a deep breath, looked at Clint and said, "So, noon tomorrow?  Where we doin' it?"

* * *

THE NEXT DAY at noon, Clint parked at the old rock quarry and waited for the Reverend Billy C. Reid to drive up with his money.  After the girl went to bed the night before, Clint and Waylon stayed up to discuss the specifics. Waylon would keep Eustice at the trailer just in case she got the idea to bolt, like maybe she'd been putting them on the whole time. Clint would meet with the Reverend, get the money and come back to the trailer. Then they'd both take the money and split, leaving the crazy girl at the trailer with just the clothes on her back. Waylon, always the softie, said they should leave her with something and Clint came back with, "Why? She's a spoiled little rich girl that can get anything she wants. Ain't nobody ever gave us nothin' in our lives. This is *our* turn." And that's all that was said about that.

Clint sat there in his Chevy pickup truck, wearing his lucky Dale Earnhardt cap over the pantyhose, running his fingers over the big three on it. He was wearing that same hat the time they bought lottery tickets up in Virginia and he scratched them off to find they won a hundred bucks. And that time he made out with Jenny Mossman out in the barn and went all the way, he never took the hat off the whole time. It was the only thing he was wearing when they finished.

He was replaying that memory, listening to the Dukes of Hazzard theme on the radio about some good ole boys never meanin' no harm, imagining that to be him and Waylon, when the Reverend Billy C. Reid drove up in a shiny black Lexus. Clint watched as the Reverend stopped beside him, facing the other way, their driver's side doors beside each other. When he was sure nobody had followed the Reverend, he opened his door and got out. So did the Reverend.

"Where's my little girl?" the Reverend said with his eyebrows drawn together, dressed in a suit like he had one of his TV sermons after they met; go straight there with Eustice and try to save her soul on national TV, telling the world what just happened to his poor little girl, crying and carrying on in front of the cameras. Eustice'd probably tell him to go to hell right there in front of everybody and he'd talk about the demons in her, how she needed everyone's prayers more'n ever now.  Their money too.

"She's safe with my brother," Clint said.  "Waitin' on me to return with the cash.  Then we'll let her go."  Clint tried to look cool leaning up against the hood of his truck, his cap pulled low on his forehead, the pantyhose smushing his nose flat.

"If you've touched her at all—"

"Relax, Reverend, ain't nobody touched her.  We been perfect gentlemen which is more'n I can say for her.  Now, where's my money?"

The Reverend leaned into his open car door and pulled a briefcase out from the passenger's side, a shiny silver one with a three-digit combination lock under the handle.  Clint's heart was beating like that time he played chicken with Brian Bigelow on Ferguson Farm Road.

Clint took the briefcase and set it on his hood, opened it, and held back the urge to scream a *yeehaa*.  He'd never seen so much money in one place before.  He wanted to count it but he figured with all those hundreds bundled together, if it wasn't three million, it was damn sure close enough.  Turning to the Reverend, he smiled and said thanks and that he'd be seeing his little girl before he knew it.  Winking as he turned around.

He hopped in his truck, threw the briefcase on the seat beside him, and turned the ignition.  It didn't crank.  He looked at the dashboard, hearing it *click-click* as he turned the key, running through his mind what could be wrong, *click-click*, breaking a sweat and looking out at the Reverend glaring back at him.

Clint stepped out of the truck, popped his hood, and said, "I need a jump."

"You need a what?"  The Reverend looked at him like he'd asked for some rosary beads and a prayer rug.

"I said I need a jump.  Back your car up and pop your hood."  Clint reached in and pulled some cables out from behind his seat, went to the front of his truck and waited for the Reverend to do what he said.

It was twenty more minutes before he got back to the trailer, happy he had the money but pissed that his truck was giving out on him.  First thing they'd have to do would be to buy a new one, maybe one with back seats, an extended cab, and a built-in tool box in the truck bed.  Get a bed liner and some Yosemite Sam mud flaps, ones with him giving the finger.

Waylon and Eustice came running out of the trailer, eyes gleaming and smiles beaming, talking a million miles a minute, saying stuff like, "Did you get it?" and "Everything go okay?" and "What took so long?"  Clint jumped out of the truck, leaving it running, and waved the briefcase around like it was first prize at the state fair for the fattest hog.

"Three million bucks!" he yelled.

"I can't believe it!" said Waylon.

"Were you followed?" the girl asked.

Clint said "Hell no" before he even thought about it.

"Are you sure?"

"Yeah."

"Really sure?  You actually look?"

Clint hesitated.  He never really checked; he was too excited.  Eustice picked up on it, saying, "Okay, let's go.  We have to get out of here.  We can divvy it up in another city."  She jumped into the truck before Clint could react.

Clint was about ready to tell the little girl to take a hike, that he and Waylon were splitting with the loot and she was *shit-out-of-luck*, but then he remembered her car at the mall, a sleek little number with a rag-top and an ignition that probably started on the first try.  He couldn't trust the truck to make it much further and if they screwed her now, they wouldn't have time to get a new one in town before the cops would be all over them.  But the girl had a car they could use to get to another town where they could buy a truck and split for good, a truck she wouldn't know what it looked like, and then they could bolt for Mexico or Canada or North Dakota and retire.

So Clint told Waylon to get in and as they drove to the mall, he told them about needing to use her car to get out of town.  Eustice thought that was funny, stealing money from her dad and then needing his help to start the getaway truck.  *Sweet justice*, she said.

In the mall parking lot, Eustice pulled a stack of money out of the briefcase and closed it again.  She threw the briefcase into the trunk of her convertible and turned to Clint and Waylon.

"I want some new clothes, right now.  I've been wearing these for three days and I won't wear them a minute more.  Let's go."

Clint didn't move.  "Now hold on a minute," he said.  "Just what the hell you think you're doin'?"

"I'm spending some of our money."

"That's not what I'm talkin' about and you know it."

"What?"  Eustice looked at him, then rolled her eyes, holding out her keys.  "Here.  Take them.  Like I care."

The brothers let Eustice drag them into stores they'd have never been caught dead in before, stores that only sold women's clothes, clothes that were tight, hip and revealing in a young fashionable way.  Stores that had stuff like you'd see advertised in one of them magazines in the grocery store aisle beside the bubble gum and candy bars.  Magazines where they always had too much makeup and spiky hair.

Then she convinced them to buy something for themselves; took them in American Eagle and picked out outfits for both of them, her saying stuff like *if she was gonna run away with them, she wanted them to look bad-ass.*

Nice clothes that Clint thought would look good on him, bring out his coolness. Maybe look like one of those actors on a Fox TV show where the young people were always screwing each other.

"Whaddya think?" Clint said as he emerged from the dressing room, the girl nowhere to be found. Waylon came out from his dressing room in his own hip clothes.

"I like it," Waylon said. "How about me?"

"Where's the girl?"

"I don't know." Waylon turned and looked at his ass in the big mirror. "I think they's too tight. What do you think?"

"Waylon, where's the girl?"

"I don't know." Then looking at Clint and understanding the question for the first time, his eyes got big and pants grew tighter.

By the time they got to the parking lot, Eustice's convertible was gone and with it, the three million bucks.

Clint stood there, dumbfounded, unable to believe this had happened. He fingered the keys in his pocket, then pulled them out and studied them. Two house keys, a garage opener and a Mickey Mouse keychain. No BMW keys. Clint threw his lucky Earnhardt cap on the pavement and kicked it. It landed a couple feet away pointing at him, the three logo dented in.

"These ain't so tight once you get 'em stretched out," Waylon said as he turned in circles, trying to get a good look at his butt.

Clint leveled his gaze at his older brother with heavy-lidded eyes, waiting a second before finally saying, "You look like a fag."

Waylon frowned but went back to trying to see what his butt looked like, spinning in slow circles and looking over his shoulder like a drunk puppy wondering what that thing shaking back there was.

They didn't find the note jammed under the hood until they got some guy with a Toyota to jump-start the truck. It read: *Thanks for a fun time fellas, I had a blast.  Sorry I had to run but I didn't feel like sharing my money.  Oh, and by the way, since you're wondering, they're bigger and firmer than you could ever imagine.  xoxoxo -Candace*

29

"There was a time when a fool and his money were soon parted, but now it happens to everybody."

*Adlai E. Stevenson*

# #2

# The Investment

THE WOMAN WAS PERFECT, dressed in designer clothes, high heels, nice hair, just a tad over forty, smelling of money.  Ryan guessed it wasn't hers though; she'd married into it.  That's what women that looked like her did.  They never earned it themselves; they stole it with a marriage certificate and a promise of amazing sex for the rest of your life.  You paid for it one way or another.

That's precisely why when he had sex, he went ahead and paid for it up front.  Not only was it easier but there were never any hidden agendas, no chance of broken promises because none were ever made.  It was the safest way.

He followed the woman from store to store, slinking behind her like a detached shadow, window shopping while she bought dresses and shoes and matching jewelry.  The smell of the sticky bun place in the food court eventually snagged her.  She probably worked out twice a day so she could eat one of them things and it not go straight to her thighs.  This would be the perfect place to do it so Ryan entered the line right behind her, imagining just how tight her thighs were, watching her backside, enjoying the way it wiggled back and forth in her expensive slacks as she moved closer to the register.

She ordered a sticky bun with strawberry glaze and a Diet Coke to wash it down, taking out her money purse from her bag, the same one she'd been paying cash from all afternoon  She handed the chick with the nose-ring a twenty because it was the smallest bill she had.  She returned the purse to her bag and as she grabbed her food, Ryan carefully reached into the bag and lifted the purse out.

He stuffed it in his Sears shopping bag he'd come in the mall with, stepped up to the counter and ordered the same thing the woman had.  Why not?  It sounded pretty good.

She sat in the food court and dropped her bags in the seat beside her, crossing her legs and resting a hand in her lap.  She ran a finger across the sticky bun and tasted it before sinking a fork in it.

Ryan knew he should keep on moving but he was strangely drawn to her, wondering what her husband was like, thinking did she like to get freaky in bed, do things you only read about in Penthouse Forum.  Ryan liked to believe that stuff was all true and wouldn't accept that it was probably all made up like his friend Troy said.

When he worked at UPS, Troy would bring in his Penthouses and pass them around.  They'd read them out loud during break; Ryan thought the stories were as good as the pictures.  But Ryan only lasted a few months there because slinging packages all day was real work and like his lazy-ass dad always said, the men in his family weren't built for real work.  Ryan tended to agree.

He plopped down at a table right across from her, facing the woman, so that when she looked up and saw him eating the same thing she was, maybe she'd smile or say something.  Sometimes bored married women liked to mess around.  They did all the time in the Penthouse letters.  Maybe he'd get lucky and score with her, write one of them nasty stories himself.

She looked up at him as he was sipping his Diet Coke.  Why the hell did he get a Diet Coke?  He didn't like that diet stuff, it was too damn sweet.  She laughed at the face he made.

Ryan returned her smile, noticing how perfect her teeth were, becoming self-conscious of his own teeth, wondering if they were as white and straight as hers were.  Then she did something that froze him in his tracks; took her finger and raked across the strawberry-glazed sticky bun, raised it to her lips, darted her tongue out and slowly licked it clean.  All while she held eye contact with him.

That's how he'd start the story to Penthouse, he thought at that moment, with her doing the finger-licking thing while staring at him from the next table.  He ran scenarios through his head as he rose and took his tray and Sears bag over and sat down at her table, right in front of her, not more than two feet from her perfect white teeth and strawberry-covered lips.

"Ryan," he said, holding out his hand, expecting her to hold hers out, then he'd take it, turn it over and kiss it lightly.  See how many points that got him.

But she didn't hold her hand out, she did something even better.  She said, "I don't care.  We don't need names for what we're going to do."

*Damn!*  He'd have to remember that line for the letter, it sounded just like what would happen to one of those guys who wrote in, just before the woman took him home to share him with her twin sister, both the girls being airline stewardesses on a week's vacation.

"And what would that be?" he said, it being the only thing he could think of seeing as how she'd caught him so off guard.

She raised her eyebrows. "If you don't know that, maybe we should call it a day right now." She started to get up with her tray, the rings on her fingers sparkling in the sunlight that poured in through the mall skylights, making Ryan wonder how much they were worth.

"Wait!" Then he said a little softer as she halted, "Wait. You just took me a little by surprise." Ryan tried to look as cool, seeing a chance to get laid by a quality piece of ass, something that doesn't happen to him every day. *Shit, something that doesn't ever happen to him.*

She sat back down, picked up her sticky bun and took a big bite out of it, giving him the eye the whole time. When she swallowed, she licked her lips sensuously, saying, "Maybe we should save these for afterward? You know, to replenish our energy."

Ryan *did* know. "I'll be right back with something to wrap 'em up with." He practically fell out of his seat as he hurried to the sticky bun place, hearing her say something about the bathroom when he turned his back.

She was still gone when he returned, her sticky bun and Diet Coke sitting on the tray where she left them. He wrapped up the food and when she still hadn't returned a minute later, he sat down to wait. He leaned back and crossed his legs, trying to look as comfortable as possible like this wasn't a big deal to him, like it happened to him all the time. *Yeah, this was gonna be one hell of a letter to write.*

He rested his arm on the back of his seat and looked around, hoping to see her, thinking about what kind of underwear she had on, wanting to see her walking his way swaying those hips of hers. He wondered what her name was, glanced around again, and decided to rifle through her wallet to find it, maybe surprise her by telling her she looked like a Diane if her name was Diane, score another point or two.

The Sears bag was empty. Not only was *her* money purse gone but the three wallets he'd lifted earlier that morning were also missing. And then, seeing that all her bags were gone, he put two and two together and closed his eyes and shook his head. Ryan pinched the bridge of his nose and breathed in slowly, then exhaled. He wasn't upset, he was disappointed. A guy didn't come by a piece of ass like that every day.

He picked up the paper sack, already stained from the sticky buns inside, dropped his Diet Coke off in the trashcan, and strolled out of the food court. In the parking lot, he saw her by a burgundy Chrysler, searching her purse with a scowl on her face.

He came up behind her, saying, "Looking for these?" He held out her keys he'd pocketed the same time he lifted her money purse, smiling as he jingled them in his right hand.

She turned around with a smirk on her flawless face, eyes twinkling like she'd just remembered a punch line from a joke someone told her a week ago. Then she said, "Slick, real slick."

He leaned up against her car, keys still in his hand. "You ain't so bad yourself, had me goin' there. You sure know how to use your assets." Ryan smiled at his joke and she held out her hand for the keys but Ryan wasn't finished yet. "So, was any of it real, any of that back there?" Motioning with his head toward the mall, knowing she knew what he meant.

She shrugged. "How much of it do you want to be real?" Still holding out her hand for her keys, Ryan not giving them up, his arms now crossed over his chest.

He smiled, seeing she wanted to keep playing. He could do that too. "So, where to?" he said as he pushed off the car, clicked the unlock button on the key chain and walked over to the passenger's side. She watched as he opened the door and hopped in, making himself comfortable, adjusting the seat to fit his long legs, the hum of the electric seat motor filling the silence.

* * *

THE MOTEL ROOM was like most he'd been in.  Lumpy bed, peeling wallpaper, coarse towels, TV bolted to the wall, five minute wait for hot water.  But more importantly, this time there was a naked woman under the sheets beside him.

Sarah.  That's what she said her name was, but Ryan didn't know if that was her real name or not.  Even if she showed him an ID, he still wouldn't believe it a hundred percent.  She didn't give him a last name.  No matter, he didn't need that anyway.

She handed him a blunt she'd taken a few puffs from, a nice big fat one that looked almost like a miniature ice cream cone.  It was good stuff, too, none of that cheap weed his buddy Willie sold, stuff he got from some Mexicans that'd moved in down the road, thirteen of them living in a two bedroom house and a building out back.  This was some of that high-grade stuff somebody grew in their basement with special lighting, sold for eight thousand a pound, could get you high and keep you there till the new year came back around.

They were past mellow now, having had sex twice, once in missionary position, once with her on top, screaming cuss words right before she hit her climax.  Damn, he was good.  Yeah, he was definitely going to write a letter to Penthouse, mention the scratch marks down his back and that thing he did with his middle finger that made her eyes cross; just thought of it right there on the spot and it worked like a charm.

"You know," Sarah said, "you really ought to step up your game."

Ryan held the blunt out to her, hesitating before asking what she meant, knowing damn well she wasn't talking about the amazing sex they'd just had. "Huh?" he said.

"Working a mall for chump change. It's bush league." She was sitting up next to him, leaning back against the headboard, holding the covers up over her tits. Ryan thought women only did that in PG movies but now, watching Sarah do it, he wondered if women covered them up because they got cold or because they were self-conscious. He wished she'd let them hang out so he could look at them any time he wanted.

"I do alright," he said.

"Yeah, sure. How much do you bring in on a good day?"

He looked up at the ceiling. "Five, six hundred. Brought in as much as two grand before, though. That's pretty good, you ask me." Remembering the time he lifted the wallet off a guy who'd been looking for an engagement ring, the guy going from jewelry store to jewelry store searching for the best deal, probably had the idea he'd get another ten percent off the final price if he offered cash on the spot. Ryan wondered what the guy did when he finally found the perfect ring, haggled an hour over the price and then went to pay for it.

Exhaling a lungful of smoke, she said with a strained voice, "Peanuts. That's nothing. I spend that in a day. You should aim your sights higher. You're not a bad looking guy; you could work some better stuff."

Taking the blunt from her, he asked, "Like what?" She had him curious now.

"Well, first, you need to reinvent yourself or you'll never be able to pull off the big con. Change your style, you know. To attract the big money, you have to look like you *have* money yourself. That means no more t-shirts and jeans, no tennis shoes, no shopping at Walmart. You have to wear expensive stuff; Hugo Boss, Versace, Christian Dior. You know, stuff like that."

Ryan almost laughed, he wouldn't be caught dead in that overpriced crap. Paying an extra fifty bucks for the label when the clothes were made in the same sweatshops in Thailand as the Walmart stuff.

"You don't believe me?" She looked at him, seeing the expression on his face. "I grew up in a singlewide in the low country, down near Charleston. All my clothes were hand-me-downs from Salvation Army and when I ran away at fourteen, I swore I'd never live like that again. Pork and beans and fried spam every day washed down with dirty well water." She paused, then changed her scowl to a smile. "But you'd never know that to look at me today would you?"

The expression on Ryan's face said it all. He knew trailer trash alright and she wasn't trailer trash. He'd grown up screwing those whores for little baggies of cheap pot, sometimes for just a six-pack of Bud Light and a half-hearted compliment. No, this woman had a high-class aura about her. She even *smelled* expensive, not like that cheap soap you got two-for-a-buck at the dollar store. And her hair was done up nice, with just enough curls to look sophisticated, not oily and grungy like the girls he'd known in the trailer park.

"So, how did you change?" he asked.

"I just *did it*, that's how. It's all up here."—pointing to her head—"It's all in your attitude and the way you carry yourself and first, you have to change that in your head. Nobody else can do that for you. You put the right clothes on and talk like a winner and suddenly you're a different person because everybody *thinks* you are."

Ryan thought about it hard, dreaming about living the good life, waking up with somebody like Sarah in his bed every day, a pair of tits like hers there to fondle any time he wanted; watch her walk around the room in nothing but a thong, see her tits sway back and forth when she fixed her hair in the mirror and put on her make-up each morning.

She got up, saying she had to pee, and he stared at her bare ass shaking as she scooted around the corner into the bathroom. She left the door open and he heard her lower the seat from where he left it up earlier. He could watch an ass like that all day long and never get bored.

"And then, when you're making some real money," she said over her tinkling, "I can introduce you to my investment guy. He'll put your money into all kinds of stuff. You get enough scores and you'll be able to live off the interest the rest of your life. Never work another day till you die."

Now she really had Ryan's attention, talking about making enough money he could sit on his ass and still never run out. That sounded pretty good to him.

"So, what kinda cons we talkin' about? What's the *big stuff?*"

He heard the toilet flush and saw her come out to the double-sink counter. "That depends on you," she said as she turned and washed her hands.

Ryan watched all the right parts of her jiggle in the big mirror on the wall, enjoying the sights, wondering if they were going to do it again before they left.

"What do you think you can pull off?" she asked.

Ryan thought about it as Sarah settled back into bed. He wasn't sure; he had never considered it before. "I don't know."

"Well, you have to begin somewhere."

"It's easier for women," he grumbled. "All you gotta do is shake your ass and tits and guys fall down to give you whatever you want." The irony wasn't lost on him.

She looked at Ryan and raised her eyebrows. "It takes more than a nice ass to talk a guy out of a million bucks."

"A million bucks?"  Ryan's eyes widened.  "You've taken somebody for a million bucks before?"

"I've done it more times than you can count."

"You're shittin' me!  How much money you got?"

"Don't you know it's rude to ask a woman that?"

"I thought you didn't ask a woman how much she weighed."

"I'd tell you my weight before I told you my bank balance."

Ryan laughed.  This woman wasn't like any he'd ever known.  She was a trip.  Sexy and smart with a sense of humor.  He leaned over and did the thing with his middle finger again, watching her eyes cross and her mouth open in a big O.

* * *

A WEEK WENT BY and the new Ryan was ready for a field test.  He woke up that morning and donned a brand new steel-gray Armani suit, a red-striped power tie, some Italian leather shoes and a pair of sleek Ray Bans.  Sarah had taken him to get a new haircut and manicure two days earlier and was working with him on how to talk and walk like a rich person.  It wasn't too hard to grasp but it was definitely different; he had to inject a cocky sureness he never had before.

His new name was Clayton Parker and he had cards printed up so that on any given day he could be a Real Estate Developer, an Investment Counselor, an International Trader or an Importer/Exporter.

There were a couple of tips that Sarah drilled into his head.  One: Always try to con the opposite sex; it's easier.  Two: Never look like you want someone's money; always make it appear like working with them may be more trouble than it's worth.  Makes you seem more important.  You gotta make them force you to take it, practically beg you to do something with their money.  Three: Once you've got them on the hook, push a sense of urgency.  If they want in, *really* want in, it's got to be now or it's too late.

Four: Just like the commercial used to say, never let them see you sweat. Nothing is ever a big deal because you got so much money you can always buy your way out of any problem. Five: Always look confident, although Ryan thought this was technically the same thing as number four, not sweating. Six: If a deal falls through, no problem, there's three other suckers around the corner just waiting for you to give them the same chance. Seven: The most important thing; everyone, whether they admit it or not, is always looking for a way to make easy money. Always.

There were lots of good places to meet marks; a cigar bar, a wine tasting, Starbucks, the gym, an elevator. The secret was to get *them* to come to *you* when you were there and the way to do that was to look the part. "Look important and you *are* important," Sarah said over and over.

His goal today was to see if he could attract a mark. Nothing more. He and Sarah went several places but he wasn't comfortable yet, couldn't get used to playing the part. Nobody paid attention to him. Sarah said it was the first day, not to get discouraged yet; it took time.

That night she had plans and Ryan figured he'd go out for a drink. They weren't married after all; in fact, he didn't know what they were. They were fucking but it wasn't a relationship, which was fine with him. He didn't need nothing like that holding him back, cramping his style. Although she definitely was one quality piece of ass.

He decided he'd go look at more quality ass and pulled into Platinum Dolls, a strip joint that was supposed to be as classy as they came. College chicks and adult stars and Grade A talent, the kind that look so good they could get you off without even going down on you in the back room for an extra fifty. He wanted to get shit-faced, maybe arrange for a quick fuck with some sweet little coed when she got off her shift. At the very least, he wanted a face full of titties all night long, see so many of them he'd dream about them when he passed out.

Starr was on the stage when he showed up, dancing to the disco song *Freak Out*, her long blonde hair tied up in pigtails, wearing knee socks and nothing else except a smile and heavy blue eye shadow. Ryan grabbed a seat next to the stage and ordered a Tom Collins from the topless waitress. It was an approved drink on Sarah's list and since he was still in his new Armani suit, he thought he'd play his part. Maybe he could impress a stripper.

Starr left the stage but not before she did an inspiring split right in front of him. Ryan gave her a standing ovation and a crisp new dollar bill for her trouble. She stuffed it in her sock because there wasn't any other place to put it.

The Tom Collins wasn't so bad, a little sweeter than he liked, not as much kick as whiskey, but still sort of tasty. Up next was a brunette number by the name of Roxie, wearing a bunch of leather and dark eyeliner, dancing to a Rod Stewart song, acting real sultry and pouty. By the end of the song, Ryan had learned a few things about Roxie: she shaved everywhere, she had extremely fake titties with nipples that never got soft and she liked her riding crop, *really* liked it.

Brianna took the stage next, a dirty blonde wearing a business suit, high heels and librarian glasses, carrying a shiny silver briefcase, her hair put up in a tight bun held together by a pencil stuck down its middle. The music started when she grabbed the pole at center stage and dropped the briefcase to the floor, kicking her leg up on the first beat of Paula Abdul's *Straight Up Now Tell Me.*

None of the girls were bad but Brianna was a true professional. With her glasses off and her hair down, she looked almost too young to be stripping, but when she began to remove her suit, Ryan changed his mind. She was a full-fledged woman, all her parts original and in perfect working order. Ryan was in lust, feeding her ones during the whole number and finally dropping a twenty on her when she finished right in front of him, her eyes smiling like she truly enjoyed her job.

She came to his table a few minutes later, a drink in her hand and a swagger in her hips. She sat and pushed the drink in front of him, adjusting the jacket of her suit to show maximum cleavage.

"What's this?" he asked with a smile.

"A Tom Collins, that's what Anna said you were drinking." She leaned back and crossed her shapely legs. "It's on me."

He wrinkled his brow. "You bought *me* a drink?"

She laughed. "You spent a fortune on me up there, it was the least I could do."

Ryan shook his head, saying, "Un-fucking-believable."

"Yeah, tell me about it. This is the first time I've ever done it, too. Don't know what came over me. Just felt like it."

Ryan stuck out his hand. "My name's … Clayton." Almost forgetting to play his part with his fake name.

Brianna smiled and shook his hand. "Candace."

"Candace? I thought it was—"

"Brianna? Nah, that's my stage name. My real name's Candace. Well, it is now. Just changed it last week."

"You changed your real name? Why? You wanted by the cops?"

"No," she laughed uneasily. "I just hated my name so I changed it; swore I'd do it the second I turned eighteen."

*Eighteen?* Ryan paused, then said, "So … what was your *real* name?"

"Oh no you don't." She shook her head. "That name's dead now and so's the little girl it belonged to. I'm Candace." She held her hands under her big tits and hefted them up.

"I'll say you are. Nice dancing by the way." Ryan felt completely at ease with the girl, confident, like he was supposed to be, like it was no big deal she was sitting with him, this barely-legal perfect ten that acted way older than she said she was.

"Thank you." Her smile seemed natural. "So tell me about yourself, Clayton. What do you do for a living?"

Ryan reached into his coat pocket, produced a card and handed it to her, saying, "Investment Counseling."

"Parker Investments LLC, Clayton Parker, CEO ... New York City ... pretty impressive. I like your suit ... mine's Armani also." She fingered her lapel.

Ryan looked at his suit jacket. "You know what I'm wearing, just like that? You can't even see a tag." Ryan hoped she couldn't tell his Rolex was fake.

Candace shrugged. "I know my clothes." She pulled her suit jacket open and gave Ryan another peek at her twins, smiling when she caught his reaction, then leaned forward and said, "You see anybody coming?"

Ryan looked around. "No, why?"

She sipped his drink. "Mmm ... that's pretty good." Noticing his amusement, she said, "Too young to drink; could lose my job if I got caught."

Ryan thought that was pretty funny, how she could be old enough to shake her tits and ass for a living, but not have a beer. "Really? They'd fire you for that?"

"Probably not but why take the chance?"

The girl on the stage now was the color of chocolate milk, her skin smooth and shiny in the spotlight, introduced with the name Coco, dancing to some hip hop song Ryan had heard on a mobile phone commercial, by Beyonce he thought. She wore athletic shorts and a basketball jersey but not for very long.

"So, you're a long way from home," Candace said.

"Business trip; here for a few days."

"You make a lot of money in your business?" Candace asked, sneaking another sip of Ryan's drink.

He smiled. "I make other people a lot of money, too." He remembered some of the lines Sarah had taught him, saying it real easy-like, still watching Coco on the stage.

"She's pretty," Candace said, following his eyes.

"What? Oh, yeah, she is." He looked at Candace. "But you're much prettier."

Candace smiled, having grabbed his attention again. "So what exactly do you do all day?"

Ryan looked into her eyes, seeing her genuine interest, thinking she'd be a good test run to try out all his new skills. *Why not?* "Well, depends on how much money a person has as to what I can do for them. The more money you got, the better the opportunities and the more the return on investment."

"That's kind of vague."

He shrugged. "The question's vague."

Candace smiled again. "Okay, what if somebody had a thousand dollars? What could you do for them?"

"Hmmm ... a thousand?" He feigned like he was thinking. "I'd tell them to keep it in their savings or buy a little bank CD. Getcha three to five percent return."

"What if they had a *hundred* thousand?"

Ryan shrugged. "A little more interesting. I'd set them up with a portfolio of seventy percent stocks, thirty percent bonds. Maybe make ten to twelve percent annually, but it really depends on how much risk they wanted to take. More risk, more reward."

Candace tipped up Ryan's drink again, paused, then said, "What if somebody had a million?"

Ryan perked up now but still tried to look uninterested. "Well, that's where we get into my specialty: private placement. With a million or more, I've got contacts that can return up to twenty percent a year."

"Twenty percent?"

"Yep, and here's the best part, it's guaranteed by the bank I work with."

"Guaranteed? A twenty percent return? But that's two hundred thousand a year."

"Yep, enough to live on pretty comfortably, wouldn't you say?"

Her eyes narrowed. "What do you get out of it?"

Ryan laughed. "Well, I get ten percent of the twenty percent, that's two percent total, taken off the top. So on a million, I'd make twenty grand, just for putting somebody's money in the right hands. Twenty thousand for an introduction. Not bad, huh?"

Candace raised her eyebrows. "Not bad at all."

"Yeah, and imagine me making a few of those introductions a month. Not a bad paycheck for yours truly." Ryan sat back, proud of himself for getting all that out just like he and Sarah practiced it. Sounded so good he almost believed it himself. "I don't really need to work any more but I love to make deals. Gets my blood pumping, you know?"

Ryan could see the look on her face, her wheels spinning like a gerbil treadmill on crack. *This shit actually worked.* If she had any real money, she'd be his. He could picture the hook hanging out the side of her mouth.

Looking at her while they talked was distracting and he wished she'd offer him a lap dance. He wanted to see her naked again, feel her rubbing that firm little body all over him. Somehow, though, asking for it now seemed kind of rude. But then again, that was how the girl made her money so would it really be so rude of him to ask?

Anna the topless waitress came by again and Ryan ordered another Tom Collins, seeing as how he'd had approximately three sips from the one Candace bought him. He was enjoying sitting there, chatting with a half-naked girl while another half-naked girl walked around getting him things. Made him feel important, like a king with his harem of lovely women. And they all treated him like he was somebody special; not like every other time he'd been in strip joints, when they treated him like a john. All those other times, he could feel their contempt for him oozing out in every word they said. It was different now, *he* was different now.

"Hey, I have to go," Candace said suddenly jumping up, her right tit almost popping out of her coat. "The manager's over there giving me the eye. If I'm not lap dancing, I'm not making him any money, and I like my job. He doesn't like me spending too much time with one customer anyway but listen, don't go anywhere. I'll be back in a while, okay?" She flashed him that million dollar smile with her perfect teeth, then opened up her suit jacket and flashed him her million dollar tits, laughing like a little girl when he stared wide-eyed at them.

Coco finished with her set, throwing Ryan a lusty look before exiting the stage into the back, walking away while shaking that healthy backside, showing she wasn't an amateur either. An Asian chick came out next, dancing to the old seventies song *Kung Fu Fighting*, her set full of Bruce Lee moves, shedding parts of her Ninja costume till all she wore was a short sash tied around her forehead. Most entertaining was an extremely high kick followed by a backwards hand stand into a—*whoa,* Ryan didn't know what to call that position but he was pretty sure the image was burned into the back of his eyes and he'd dream about it later.

He was just getting comfortable when Candace appeared again, a grin on her face and a devious gleam in her eyes. "Hey, I'm back but I can't stay unless I give you a lap dance because my manager's still watching me.  Is that okay?"

Ryan thought that was about the dumbest question he'd ever heard, *Could she get naked and rub all over him?*  "Yeah, sure," he choked out as he put his drink down.

Candace intercepted it and took a swallow, then set it on the table, grabbed his chair and swung it around for easy access.  *Funky Cold Medina* blared out of the speakers.  If Ryan had a nickel for every time he heard *that* one in a strip joint … but this time was different; this time he had Candace, a little blonde vixen, rubbing her practically naked body all over him.

Topless now, she nuzzled her backside into his crotch and said over her shoulder.  "Remember, no touching."  This was the single most frustrating rule in a strip joint Ryan had ever heard of, thinking that very thought as she pressed her firm little ass into his woody and rubbed it up and down to the beat, then her saying over her shoulder again, "Mmm … I was beginning to wonder if you were straight."

*What the fuck?*  Ryan no longer paid attention to her grinding on him, wondering instead what he was doing to make her think he was gay.  It had to be the manicure; he'd fought Sarah on that one but eventually gave in to her.  "What makes you say that?" he finally asked.

Candace turned sideways and sat on his lap with her leg running all the way up his arm, wearing those thigh-high stockings with the lace around the edges.  She rested her calf on his shoulder, her business skirt opening all the way now, giving him a glimpse of her neatly trimmed money-maker, then said to him as calmly as if she were doing the dishes, "Well, I don't know, just the fact that you haven't tried to paw all over me yet."  Bringing her other leg up on the other side of his head, resting it on his other shoulder, thrusting her treasure island toward his face.  "And most all guys who come in here don't miss a chance to cop a cheap feel the first chance they get."

She wiggled and undulated back and forth like her thing was having a conversation with him, giving him directions how to get to the 7-Eleven down the street.

Ryan finally came back with, "Yeah well, I'm not most guys." That being the best he could think of with that coochie shaking in his face, smelling like baby powder and being about the prettiest thing he'd seen since he was eighteen in the back seat of his 1978 Buick Skylark Coupe with Linnie May Dobson. The car had a 5.7 liter V8 with a 4-barrel carburetor and was matched in noise and power only by Linnie May.

Candace brought her legs down and straddled him, shoving her big titties in his face, almost suffocating him as she grabbed his hair and buried his head right between them. "I can tell that," she said. "You're a lot more sophisticated than the rednecks that usually come in. It's a nice change."

"Mmmfph."

"So, let me ask you a question," she continued. "If I knew somebody who had a bunch of money, you could help them invest it and make that twenty percent you were talking about?"

She let him breathe, pulling his head out of there but still riding him like he was a pony at a five year old's birthday party, not giving him a single moment to think clearly. "Yeah, sure," he said, still concentrating on breathing normally.

"How soon could you meet with someone? I mean, like, do you have appointments through the week or how do you do it?" She ran her fingers through his neatly combed hair, mussing it up while she took one of his earlobes into her mouth and bit it lightly, then ground into him with her happy place.

"Tomorrow, I guess. I could meet tomorrow." He couldn't really think that far ahead to know if anything was happening then but tomorrow sounded good when it came out.

She said, "Great!" Then stood and turned around, finally removing that pesky business skirt by bending all the way over at the hips, pulling it down to her ankles and stepping out of it, then parting her legs and saying to him between them, "So would they come by your office or meet you for lunch or what?"

He looked at her upside-down, throwing his balance all out of whack, making him want to show her that thing with his middle finger that'd impressed Sarah so much, the blood flow running away from his brain. "Uh, yeah."

"Yeah?  Yeah what?"

"Yeah."

* * *

THEY MET FOR LUNCH the next day at La Bamba, a Mexican place that gave away hot tortilla chips and pureed salsa while you waited for your meal.  After telling Sarah about his possible deal, she went with him that morning to buy a new suit, an expensive one.  Then she coached him on what to expect and how to react to different scenarios up until the moment he left.

Candace arrived in jeans and a pullover sweater, looking totally different than the night before, looking more like a kid now than ever.  *How does this little girl know someone with a million bucks?*

"Tequila Sunrise," she ordered from the waiter, a Mexican with dark skin and scraggly mustache who spoke broken English and nodded a lot, smiling like he was speaking cuss words to them and they couldn't understand a word.

"Just a Coke for me," Ryan said.

"You don't want a real drink?" Candace asked.

He shook his head.  "No, not when I'm doing business.  Like to keep a clear head."

She shrugged, then ordered a combo three, the one with the chile rellenos stuffed with meat and cheese. Ryan ordered a number eleven, the same one he always got, with a taco, burrito and enchilada.

"So tell me how this works," Candace began when the waiter left.

"Well, shouldn't we wait on your friend?"

She looked confused, then smiled. "*I'm* the one with the money."

"You?" Ryan tried not to sound surprised or disappointed but it was too late. "I thought … look, don't take this the wrong way but I only deal with big money. That way I don't run myself crazy making a hundred bucks here and there."

She leveled a gaze at him with steady, experienced eyes. "Three million not enough for you?"

Ryan tried not to choke, wishing now he'd ordered that drink Candace was talking about. "Three million? You have three million bucks? From stripping?"

"Yep, I got three million and nope, not from stripping." She scrunched the left side of her face up and said, "Let's just say I inherited it early."

Their drinks arrived along with the chips and salsa. Ryan emptied half his glass in the first swallow. Candace sipped on her Tequila Sunrise, nibbling at a chip she dipped in the salsa.

"Inherited early? What's that mean?"

"It's a long story. Why, does it matter where I got it?"

Ryan thinking, then saying, "No, not really."

"Good, now tell me how all this works."

Ryan leaned back and tried to relax. "Well, with that much we can go straight to a bank debenture trading program, buying U.S. T-Bills at a discount and selling them retail price through the bank. Ten year notes." He hoped he was getting this right like Sarah went over with him, thinking even if he got a little bit of it wrong that Candace would never know anyway.  "It gets complicated.  Let me just say that the bank can guarantee the profit margin before they even use your money because they have a contract to sell the bills before they go and buy them.  So they know exactly what's going to be made and it's a hundred percent safe.  And of course, they get *their* fees."  He winked and smiled at her, a trick Sarah had shown him when talking about the bank getting their money.  It always made the other person agree and smile back, and Candace followed suit perfectly.

"And when do we do this?"

"Well, you're in luck there, they always do them on the twentieth of every month and today's the eighteenth so I can get it in to my contact just in time if you wanted to get started right away.  Otherwise you'd have to wait another month."  He frowned like this would be a bad thing.  Right on cue, she frowned at the same time, signaling she thought it would be a bad thing too.  "What bank do you have it in right now?" he asked.

"I don't.  It's cash."

"Cash?"  Ryan had a hard time hiding his surprise.  "You have three million in cash?  Just laying around your house?  What, you got it stuffed under your mattress or something?"

Candace smiled.  "I have it hidden but I can get to it if I need to."

"You mean to tell me that you've got that kind of cash and you're stripping for a living?"

Candace still smiling.  "I like stripping.  No, I *love* stripping, the power it gives me.  With this body I can control any man I want to and I think it's fun to watch them trip all over themselves to—"

"Clayton?"  A woman dressed in a smart-looking pants suit stopped at their table.  "Hi, how have you been?  Haven't seen you in a few weeks."  She was smiling from ear to ear, holding her arms out to him.

"Sherri, hi, I'm doing great, you know how business is."  He stood and gave her a little hug, matching her smile with one of his own.  Then turned to Candace.  "I'm sorry, Candace this is Sherri MacEntire, she's a Business Consultant with First Union."

"I hope Clayton's buying your lunch as much money as *he's* got," Sherri said as the women shook hands.

"Oh stop, Sherri.  She's not a date, she's a customer."

"Oh?  Well, you're in good hands then, and I'd *still* make him pay for lunch.  He can afford it and besides, he'll just write it off anyway."  She smiled like she'd made a funny joke.  "Well, I've got to be going, see you soon?"

"Yeah, yeah, I'll probably be in there tomorrow."

Sherri left and Ryan sat back down at the table just as their meals arrived, shaking his head and rolling his eyes, like he couldn't believe some people.

"She's interesting," Candace said, looking at him with amused eyes. "You fucking her?"

Ryan's raised his eyebrows, not believing he heard what he just heard from this girl, then he recovered.  "Her?  No, but I can tell she wants it. Been after me ever since she got separated from her husband.  She's a gold digger and I'm not into that."  Proud of himself for his little impromptu story.

"Hmm ... well, do you have any forms for me to sign, anything I can read that explains all this a little better?"

"Sure, here you go."  Ryan reached inside the briefcase he'd brought and handed her a package of paper.  "This is a small prospectus explaining the deal and how it works:  what you get out of it, my commission, the bank's fees.  Everything you want to know.  Couple of forms in the back you'll need to sign:  a confidentiality agreement, a loan agreement, a commissions statement ... you'll see it all."

"A loan agreement?"

"Yeah, what they actually do is give you a loan with your three million as a down payment, probably do it at ten percent, so your loan will be for maybe thirty million leveraged, then—"

"Thirty million?"

"Yeah, hold on, I'm getting to it.  They take that thirty million and go make like a half percent profit off it at a time, in your name … that's like a hundred fifty thousand a pop … and it quickly adds up.  That half a percent of thirty million is like five percent of your original three mil.  They promise you a twenty percent return so basically, they do this four times in the next year and you've got your return.  Then they pay the loan off with the same money and charge you fees on it, usually a point, and give you what's left over."

Candace tried to add it up in her head.  "That's … um … "

"Six hundred thousand minus my sixty thousand commission minus the bank's thirty thousand fee leaves you five-ten free and clear.  Plus your original three mill.  It's up to you to pay taxes on the income."  Sarah was right, Ryan thought, this stuff got easier each time you told it.  He was glad she'd made him run through it twenty times this morning.  When you talked big numbers like this, really big numbers, people's heads began to spin and he could see it happening with Candace now.

Conversation turned to what each of them liked to do in their spare time.  Candace was thinking of going to college now that she was out on her own, attracted to the freedom of the college lifestyle.  Remembering some of Sarah's teaching, to lie as little as possible, Ryan told her about loving to fish and playing softball and just hanging out.  He was basically lazy at heart and that's why he loved this business so much, it allowed him to bum around when he wasn't working.  Sounded good to say, too.

Later that afternoon, when he was boffing Candace from behind, watching her tits bouncing in the full length mirror on the wall, he thought of some other things he liked to do.  Play the guitar, watch old cartoons on Nickelodeon, go to drag races.

He left her with the advice to read everything over carefully and sign where he had marked, they'd meet tomorrow morning for breakfast at Denny's.  He'd buy her a Grand Slam as they finalized everything.

* * *

BREAKFAST WENT OFF without a hitch, Candace bringing in the bogus documents, having signed everywhere she was supposed to, hauling in the three million in the same briefcase that she'd used in her act two nights before.  They both had Grand Slams and Ryan left with her money and the promise that he'd call that afternoon to verify that everything was finished and set into motion.

The only call Ryan was going to make was to Sarah's investment guy.  If Sarah was right about him, the guy could get Ryan six percent a year for real, and six percent on three million was a nice little hunk of change.  Of course, he figured he'd blow a couple hundred thousand first; buy a new car and a condo at the beach, then get the rest to the guy and see what he could do with it.

He went straight to Sarah's hotel room, knocking on the door with a big fat grin on his face and a briefcase full of money in his hand.  She answered in just a towel.  Perfect.  He was in the mood to celebrate and Candace notwithstanding, Sarah was still one quality piece of ass.  And besides, he was still young enough to enjoy bagging two hot chicks in one day.

"Got it," he said when she let him in, holding the briefcase out in front of him.

She smiled and gave him a wet hug, pulling him to the bed and telling him she wanted him inside her right that moment, not to even worry with taking off his clothes, his two thousand dollar suit with the hundred dollar silk power tie.  She fumbled with his zipper, letting her towel loosen, giving him a peek of what was to come, getting him hard almost before he could pull out his soldier.

Twenty minutes of pumping and grinding and sweating and she got off three times while he tried to prolong it because it always felt better when he did that but then she did that thing with her middle finger and he lost it, his orgasm coming in waves and his eyes rolling up into his head. *Jesus Christ Almighty!* He was going to have to remember that move for sure. It had never been that intense before, making him feel as high and lightweight as a hot air balloon.

His body flooded with pleasure and he laid back to relax, thinking about everything he was going to spend his new money on. Maybe he'd only give the investment guy two million, keep a million out to play with. Get a guitar. He always wanted a guitar. Maybe …

* * *

RYAN AWOKE to the hum of the wall heater and the low volume of the TV. The weather girl was talking about tomorrow's weather being chilly in the mid fifties, odd for this time of year, the girl laughing and saying, "Back to you, Phil." Ryan opened his eyes groggily, still feeling light-headed and giddy, endorphins occupying every square atom of his body. He was lying on his side with his thing hanging out his zipper, that two thousand dollar suit still on and getting wrinkled. *Fuck it,* they'd get it dry-cleaned, something he'd never done in his life. He'd always wondered how they could clean something without actually getting it wet, wanted to know what the trick was, thinking he'd ask the clerk when they dropped it off.

He reached over for Sarah but touched only bed, then sat up and looked around. "Sarah?"—looking toward the bathroom, then saying it louder— "Sarah?"

He got up and shook the groggy from his body, saw the bathroom was empty and looked around to make sure her things still there. They were.

Then he glanced at the briefcase sitting on the table, right where he threw it when she attacked him earlier. He remembered what she did at the mall and he ran over to it, popped the clasps and opened the top.

*Nothing!* Goddammed empty space. Not even any lousy lint. He could still smell the money that used to be inside. "Fuck!!!!" He ran to the door and flung it open. An overweight Mexican maid stood there with her cart, getting ready to knock on the door; now she was smiling at him 'cause his Johnson was still peeking through his open fly. She raised her eyebrows in question, looking from his crotch up to his face, and started to say something.

"Excusay, señora," a voice beside the maid said as Sarah pushed by her. Then, "What the fuck? You advertising?"

"What? No ... " Ryan pulled it back in his pants and zipped up.

Sarah pushed her way into the room, saying, "No disturbay" to the maid as she closed the door. She looked at Ryan. "Then what the fuck are you doing'?"

"Me? Where's the fuckin' money?" Motioning his head toward the open briefcase.

"Relax," she said with a frown on her face, handing him a Coke, holding a Diet Coke in her other hand. "I just went to get some sodas. Money's over there." Looking toward a huge Macy's bag on the dresser.

Ryan ran over and yanked it open, seeing all those hundreds bundled together, heaped on top of each other, the most beautiful sight in the whole world next to that stripper's cute little snatch. He turned and said, "Why'd you take it out of the briefcase?"

"Geez. Slow down, you're going to have a fucking coronary. You want the briefcase, you can have it. I counted it all and put it in something that won't attract as much attention. You know there are some Bearer Bonds in there? Doesn't matter, we have an appointment with my investment guy in about two hours."—looking at her watch—"You want to take it in the briefcase, that's up to you, but I was going to wear jeans today and I figured you might want to get out of that suit and into something more comfortable too.  The briefcase will stand out too much where we're going."

Ryan sat on the edge of the bed now, staring at the green paisley wallpaper, finally relaxing a little, thinking his other clothes were back at his place but saying, "Oh … oh, okay.  Yeah, sure, jeans.  Yeah."

"What did you think, I was going to take off with the money?"

Ryan looked at her, the energy sucked from his system, thinking of when they met at the mall, the whole scenario looping through his mind like an endless film.

She said, "Honey, you're worth more to me as a partner."

"Partner?  We're partners now?"

Sarah peeled her shirt off.  "Sure.  And I'm taking a twenty percent cut of everything you do while we're together."

He raised his head.  "Oh yeah?  Twenty percent?"

"Yeah, if I'm going to teach you the big con, I have to get something out of it besides sex."

Ryan frowned.  "What, the sex ain't good enough?"

"Oh, the sex is great."  She smirked as she kicked off her shoes and slid out of her jeans.  "But business is business and if I'm going to be your teacher, I get twenty percent for my trouble."

"And when did we decide that?"

She laughed and walked over to the bed, pushing him onto his back and straddling him.  She leaned over so their lips were inches apart and said, "When I decided you were worth more to me as a partner than a mark."

FOLLOW THE MONEY

63

"Virtue has never been as respectable as money"

*Mark Twain*

64

# #3

# Sammy's Night Out

ALL SAMMY JOHNSON NEEDED when he went into the Scotsman was a pack of condoms. The ribbed kind 'cause Joleen said they really did feel better than the regular kind. And not to get the ones that were lubricated; that stuff messed with her system. Did the opposite of what it was supposed to do. Dried her out.

And while Sammy was at it, he was going to get a can of that Red Bull, see if it really gave him wings, let him and Joleen go all night long. Maybe get her one too. And a Snickers for later, 'cause it really satisfies, like the commercials said. And maybe one of them pink carnations they sold in the little jar by the register, for Joleen. Show her he cared.

He went in to get a three dollar pack of condoms and ended up with almost ten bucks worth of stuff. Damn place was worse than the Walmart's.

A fat lady wearing short shorts and sandals was in front of him, putting all her cottage cheese out there for everybody to see like she was showing off.  She had a bunch of crap in her flabby arms, twice as much as he had, hell, *more'n that*.  Potato chips and milk and orange juice and deodorant and toothpaste and a box of Strawberry Pop Tarts.  *Damn.  She need a fucking cart at a convenience store?*

All that was missing was a screaming two year old that wanted a stupid plastic toy she wouldn't let him have, then slap him around and tell him to shut up or she's going to knock him into next Wednesday.  Then it'd be just like the Walmart's.

The lady turned around like she forgot something, maybe garbage bags or tampons or batteries, and Sammy saw her nipples poking out her thin shirt.  *Holy Shit!*  Them things were the size of the hubcaps on his 280z.  She wasn't wearing a bra and she should've been, trip over them if she wasn't careful.

The old man in front of her left with his pack of cigarettes and she waddled up to the counter and dropped all her crap onto it.  A Snickers fell to the floor and Sammy knelt to get it; the last thing he wanted to see was her bent over showing him things that'd stunt his growth.

He held the candy bar out to her fat stubby fingers and she said thanks, her breath smelling like Doritos.  She had a voice he'd swear he heard on one of them late night ads for a 900 number.  *Singles in your area just waiting to get to know you.*  Ninety-nine cents a minute gave you a chance to get laid over the phone.  *Yeah, with a fatty.*

Her having a Snickers and him having a Snickers didn't feel right; gave him a creepy feeling, like when you show up at work one day with your mullet in a ponytail sporting a Fu-Manchu mustache and the guy you hate most—the one that's always got oil on his face like he just rebuilt an entire engine when all he's done is change the stupid timing belt—has come in with the same look. Makes you want to shave and cut your hair you spent two years growing out, just 'cause somebody'll say both of you look like brothers. And the truth is, you wouldn't piss on the guy if he was on fire.

Sammy thought maybe now he should get a Zero bar, with that white chocolate, something a little different. But he had his mind set on a Snickers. Fifth Avenue's got that peanut butter in it. Same with Butterfinger. Three Musketeers are good but too fluffy, not filling enough. Maybe they got some of them Whatchamacallits; he ain't seen them in a long time. Wonder if they still made them? Nah, he'd stick with the Snickers, keep it simple. Anyway, he was next in line, practically there, once the fat lady finished with her monthly grocery shopping.

At a convenience store. The place is for convenience, not buying everything you needed for your damn house. You get the same crap half that price at the Walmart's, if you just got off your lazy ass to drive there.

The Walmart's parking lot was too big, was probably why she didn't do that; too far for her fat ass to walk. Chafe those thunder thighs of hers. Joleen better not ever get that fucking big or she'd be out on her damn ass. All two hundred pounds of it.

No sir. Joleen better stay one-twenty and fit. He'd allow her to get to one-thirty, maybe one-forty when she was pregnant. But then she better lose that fucking weight when she spit the kid out, and lose it pronto.

The fat lady finally paid for her stuff and was waddling out of the store the same time a dude came in waving around a gun like he hadn't had his meds that day. "Alright everybody, this a fuckin' hold-up!" Yelling like anybody with a third grade education couldn't figure it out by themselves.

*Damn*, Sammy thought, he needed this like he needed a fat ass chick in his bed.

The guy with the gun didn't look too old, white guy maybe in his early twenties. Hard to tell 'cause he hadn't shaved in a few days and his eyes were bloodshot and surrounded by dark circles. *Strung out* was the first thing Sammy thought. Crack, maybe meth. No, the way the guy was darting his eyes all around, then looking out the door, then back again, it was crack. Sammy'd had some of that shit before; never again. Made you paranoid as fuck and didn't last long enough. Ten minutes after a hit and you wanted more, *needed* more. Sammy wasn't made of money like that.

No, pot was his drug of choice. Nice and mellow, last all night, never get sick, never get wigged out, and could get it at a pretty good price when you bought it in bulk like he did. Had this nice water bong made out of some plastic two liter Coke bottles. Took all the harshness out. Smooth as all get out.

The dude was yelling at everybody to shut the fuck up, which Sammy thought was pretty funny 'cause the dude was the only one talking. Pointing his gun now at the fat lady and telling her to back the fuck up real nice and slow. Sammy didn't think she had any speed but slow. Yeah, he thought that was pretty funny and wanted real bad to say it out loud but he didn't think anybody'd get it. Or, at least, they wouldn't laugh with a gun in their faces.

The fat lady, a grocery bag in each arm, backed up real nice and slow just like the dude said. Sammy wanted to make a beeping sound like a garbage truck makes when it's in reverse. *God, that would be funny.* He wished Joleen were here; he'd do it then and she'd get it, think it was funny as hell and laugh out loud, gun or not.

There were three other people in the store: a teenager that looked like he'd just come off his learner's permit, an old woman with poofed out gray hair and thick glasses, and a guy with a business suit on, probably worked late at his office and just got off.

The dude with the gun was jerking his head back and forth, spinning around and trying to look everywhere at once. Sammy wondered if he'd ever done this before, stuck up a place, 'cause he didn't look too sure of himself.  But then again, the dude was jacked out of his mind.  That crack shit could fuck with you pretty good.  Sammy'd seen lots of guys get hooked on it and sell their car, steal from their mama, hell, even try and trade their old lady's snatch for a single hit that lasted no more than an hour.

The dude, at the counter now, pointed his gun at the store clerk, a ratty-looking older woman with stringy hair and half her teeth.  She looked like the type that could be strung out on some drugs herself; the kind'll suck a guy off for a forty-rock.  Hell, probably get you off for a twenty, at least a handjob or something.

"Don't try no funny shit," he told her, "Don't trip no alarms or try to pull a gun out."

*What's he thinking, she give a damn if the Scotsman Company loses a few bucks?  As if she's gonna do something stupid like try and stop him.  Dude's really high on crack, he thinks that.*

"Open the cash register and gimme it all."

The dude waved his gun at her face, holding it sideways like he'd seen on some bullshit rap video.  Waving it not more than three feet from Sammy.  The dude was making all kinds of stupid errors; definitely an amateur.  Sammy could teach him a thing or two.

"What the fuck you lookin' at?"  The dude turned his glazed eyes toward Sammy.  Sammy held eye contact, even when the dude swung his gun around and pointed it at *his* face.  Sammy held steady while the dude shook like a ninety year old man picking up his Viagra at the drugstore.

"I said, what the fuck you lookin' at?"

Sammy thought, *why the hell not tell him a thing or two?*  He sniffed and shifted his feet, then said, "I'm lookin' at you fuck up a simple robbery."

"What?"  The dude opened his eyes wide like it was dark and he couldn't see well.  "I ain't fuckin' nothin' up."

"Sure you are.  Wanna know how?"

The dude darted his eyes around the place, thought about it a second as his stomach growled, then said, "Yeah."

"First of all, this place ain't never got no real money in it.  Don't you read the stickers on the door?  Stickers that say the place ain't got more'n fifty dollars in the register at any time.  Stickers supposed to dissuade you from trying to hold the place up."  Sammy was glad he could get that word, *dissuade*, in there.  A big word made him sound smart, like maybe he'd gone farther than eleventh grade in high school.

"Huh?"

Sammy had him now.  "Most the money's in the safe."

"Safe?"

Sammy rolled his eyes.  "Yeah, the safe.  Place like this got a good safe."

The guy wiped his nose with his gun hand and looked at the woman behind the counter, then back at Sammy.

"Second, you didn't even ask her to go under the tray to get the big bills.  That's where the money is.  What's in the bag, couple bucks in fives and ones?  Maybe a few tens?"

The dude looked at the paper bag sitting on the counter the woman had put there.  She even creased the top twice, rolling it over neatly while Sammy was talking.  The dude grabbed the bag with his free hand and tried to open it but the creases were pretty good.  He ended up tearing the bag before he got into it 'cause he didn't want to put his gun down.  He rooted around in it, straining his neck and bloodshot eyes, then said, "Ain't nothin' bigger'n a ten in here."

"Told ya."

He aimed the gun at the clerk's head again and said. "You tryin' to cheat me?  You didn't give me all the money.  I said to gimme all the money."

"Calm down, dude," Sammy said as he stuck his hands in his front jeans pockets, trying to look casual and cool so the dude wouldn't lose it and start shooting everybody.  "She's just doin' her job, man, what she was trained to do.  Dig?"

The dude looked at Sammy, understanding what he was saying 'cause he looked back at the woman and said, "You trained to do that?  Just gimme the small bills?  That what you trained to do?"

The clerk nodded and said yeah, looking sleepy-eyed like she was ready for the dude to leave so she could get on with her night.  She'd have to call her manager and the police and spend all that time doing bullshit things and filling out bullshit forms she wasn't getting paid to do before she could go home and crash.

Sammy was having fun now.  He said, "Ask her to lift up the tray and hand you the big bills."

The dude swiveled toward her and said, "Yeah, do what he said."

"No, don't," Sammy said.  Then the guy looked at him wondering what the hell was going on.  Sammy said to the dude, "I told you, you gotta *ask* her, not tell her.  Don't you know you get a lot farther in this world when you act nice?"

The dude looked pained, like he got gas after eating Mexican, all those beans in everything they make.  He said, "I'm holdin' the fuckin' place up, man. I ain't *gotta* be nice.  I got a fuckin' gun."  Waving it around sideways trying to make a point.

Sammy shrugged.  "I'm just tryin' to help, dude.  I give you any bad advice yet?  Told you about the big bills when you're gettin' ready to walk outta here with a bag full of air.  I steer you wrong yet?"

The dude sucked in a deep breath and blinked his eyes rapidly, processing what Sammy was telling him. Sammy urged him with his head to go on. "Alright, alright!" then dude said, looking at the clerk. "Can you *please* gimme the rest of the money, the twenties and shit?" He put an emphasis on the word, *please*, like he was being made to do something horrible, like eat a second helping of collard greens and fatback.

Then the guy looked back at Sammy for approval. Sammy said, "It was better but you didn't sound like you meant it."

"I didn't."

"And that's why it sounded like it."

All the while, the clerk was stuffing the big bills in the bag and the fat lady was still holding her groceries. Probably the most exercise she'd gotten all week and couldn't wait to get back to her doublewide to catch up on Springer and Wheel of Fortune.

"Okay, now," the dude said. "Where's the safe?"

"Geez," Sammy said. "Are you a total dumbshit?"

The dude looked at him surprised, not believing Sammy just said that, him being the one with the gun and all. Finally saying, "What?"

"Look, dude. She can't get in the safe. This your first fuckin' time holdin' a place up?"

"Whaddya mean she can't get in the safe? How she put the money in when she takes it outta the register? Huh?" The dude raised his eyebrows and pursed his lips together, acting like he asked a good question.

"Jesus Christ, dude, you don't know *shit* do you?" Sammy paused a second while that sank in. Then said, "There's a slit in the top of the safe where she drops the bills in. She don't got the combination; only the manager got that."

The dude looked at the woman clerk. "That true? What he said? You don't got the combination?"

She nodded, still looking sleepy-eyed, like if she had a pillow she'd lay down right now, put her head on the counter and knock out 'cause she'd been on her feet all day.

"Fuck!" the guy exploded so loud that everybody in the place jumped but Sammy.

"Yeah, not a good trade, dude. You come in here, wave your gun around, gonna rob a fuckin' convenience store, be a big job. Right? *Wrong.* You know how much time an armed robbery gets in this state?" When the dude didn't answer, Sammy said, "Ten years minimum. That's like a Class B felony or some shit like that. You don't get no community service for no shit you use a *gun* on."

"You don't get nothing you don't get caught." The dude smiled with his yellow teeth, nodding his head, looking around at everyone like he was a comedian on stage and had just delivered a real dinger.

"Man, see what I mean? You a total *dumbshit.* You ain't even asked us to empty *our* pockets." Sammy waving at all the customers in the store. "Course, none of us look like we got nothing anyway. Nothing more than a few bucks, 'cept maybe the guy in the suit back there. But no, then again, he looks like a credit card man. Probably don't carry no cash at all on him. But what I'm gettin' at, dude, is that you're already caught."

"What? What you mean?" The guy's eyes darted out the store windows and back again.

Sammy closed his eyes, shook his head and opened them back up. "Look up, to your left. See that? Smile real big cause you're gonna be on the news tonight. Shit, they'll be showing this video on World's Dumbest Criminals. Headlines in the paper'll be 'Man Gets Ten Years For Eighty Bucks.' You didn't think of that did you?"

The dude was getting nervous again, looking around paranoid like there were cops already outside waiting to run in and bust him. Looking like he was going to have a heart attack 'cause things weren't working out like he'd planned.

"Look, I got an idea," Sammy said, wanting to help the dude out. "If you willing to listen."

"Yeah. What? What is it?" He was waving his gun around and starting to look like he needed that crack hit real bad.

"Geez, man, calm the fuck down why don't you. Here's the deal. I'm pretty sure none of us care that you robbin' the store." Sammy once again waving his arms around the place, everybody shaking their head *no* in their own way, expressions blank and tired. "And I'm pretty sure she don't give a fuck either." Pointing at the clerk, her shaking her head *no*, too. "But look, you walk outta here with that money, she's gotta report it or she gets in trouble. Maybe loses her job and shit. She gots no choice. But, now listen to me, if you gave her the money back then she wouldn't have no reason to call the police. Understand?"

The dude looked back at her, thinking about the whole deal, then said, "You'd do that? Forget about it just like that?"

She shrugged. "Yeah, sure." Her teeth looked like they were going to fall out, crooked and blackened on the edges where cavities had taken over.

The dude lowered the gun, seeing a way out now. Maybe thinking of celebrating at Red Lobster, get one of them shrimp specials they're always advertising on TV. Then, getting agitated again, he said, "What about the video? They still got me on video." He pointed his gun at the little security camera.

"Think about it," Sammy said, bringing a finger to his temple. "They don't ever look at that thing till something happens and if you give the money back, then nothin's really happened. *Right? Am I right?*" He looked at the clerk and she nodded.

"Really? They don't look at it if nothin's happened?"

"Ain't that what I said?  Think about it, dumbshit.  If you were a store manager, would you look at it every day if nothin' happened?  *Well?*"

The dude shook his head slowly.

"Alright then, there you go."  Sammy smiled now like he'd just solved the world's oil problem.  "Ten years worth a few lousy bucks?"  The dude was still shaking his head no as Sammy continued, "Not to me neither, man.  Me neither."

He paused while the guy stood there with a wild look on his face, his eyes not necessarily focusing on the same thing his brain was.

"So whatcha waitin' on?"

The dude looked unsure now, not certain he wanted to give the money back.  Maybe thinking about it a little bit more before he finally put the paper bag back on the counter and said, "Here, I'm givin' it back.  Put it back where you got it."

"There you go, man.  There you go.  That wasn't so hard now was it?"  Sammy said to comfort the dude.  "Now, you walk out that door and you a free man.  Don't gotta worry 'bout nothin', do he?"  Sammy glanced over at the clerk who was busy putting the money back in the register, her shaking her head *no*, that greasy hair moving so much it was beginning to piss Sammy off.  Maybe he'd tell her she needed some conditioner while he was on a roll.  Get her some of that White Rain at the dollar store.

Then the guy backed out slowly, still with the gun in his hand like somebody was going to try something on him, but not pointing it or waving it around like when he first came in, just kind of held out in front of him.  *What a complete dumbshit.*

Sammy stepped up to the counter, put his stuff down and waited to be rung up.  Nobody else moved at first, not sure that what just happened really happened at all, what they should do next.  The fat lady, still holding her bags, shrugged and left to go home to her skinny husband.

Sammy wondered why is it those really fat women, the ones whose thighs that fight to get around each other when they walk, why is it they always have these skinny men with them? That bothered Sammy. Fat women should have fat men in their lives. What did the skinny men get out of the relationship?

"Eight thirty-four," the clerk said.

*Hmm ... gettin' out cheaper than I thought, cool.* Sammy pulled out a wad of bills held together with a thick rubber band. The clerk looked at him, looked at the handful of money in his hand, watched him peel a twenty off, and laughed, showing Sammy her rotted out teeth and dark red tongue.

"You had that the whole time?" she said.

"Yep." Sammy smiled 'cause during it all, he didn't even think about it. He was used to tellin' everybody he didn't have nothing. Then the guy in the suit started laughing 'cause he saw what was going on, the teen joining him, and finally the old lady, her Coke-bottle glasses sliding down her nose. Them all laughing at Sammy and his huge bundle of money.

The money was from a sheetrock job he'd done under the table for some rich guy; he was planning on taking Joleen somewhere special for her birthday. Maybe some vacation at a theme park like Tweetsie Railroad. Or maybe take her gambling to the Indian casino and make believe they were big spenders for a weekend. Get treated like royalty or something. At least get a bunch of free drinks while they gambled.

Then the irony hit Sammy right smack between the eyes. He couldn't wait to get home to tell Joleen all about it and follow it up by whipping out his wad of money, wait for her to see it and start laughing. The dude was probably driving home right now, geeking out behind the wheel, still no money to score drugs with. It was pretty damn funny, now that the dude wasn't waving the gun in Sammy's face any more.

He should have told the dude he had the safety on just to see him wig out; but then again, he probably would have shot someone while he was messing with it. Maybe Sammy'd tell Joleen he told the dude about the safety and the dude clicked it the other way, actually clicking it on instead of off. The dude was so geeked out he might've done it. It'd make the story funnier. Yeah, he'd do that, tell Joleen the whole thing about the safety like it really happened that way.

The next morning, Sammy read in the paper about a shooting at a Circle K just down the road from the Scotsman. Seems some dude came in to rob the place and the guy behind the counter pulled out a shotgun and let him have it square in the chest. Dude bled to death before the ambulance got there. Story said the gunman asked politely for the money while waving his gun like a wild man.

Sammy didn't care. *Stupid dumbshit made him forget Joleen's carnation.* Sammy really wanted to get it for her, set the mood for when he got home. It was supposed to be a special night, seeing as how he'd got the ribbed condoms and Red Bulls and Snickers. But he forgot the pink carnation, so it wasn't that special. Sometimes it was the little things that mattered.

"Money often costs too much."

*Ralph Waldo Emerson*

# #4

# A Loaded Gun

"HOW ABOUT THAT ONE?" Junior said, sniffing his nose and jerking his head around, nodding toward a champagne-colored Honda Accord.

"Nah," Calvin said, walking beside him, looking around the parking lot coolly, keeping his hands in his pockets, his cap pulled low on his head. "I want an American one. They're easier."

"That one?"

Calvin stopped and looked at Junior. "That's a Mercedes. I said American."

"But I like that one."

"It's too hard to get into."

"But it's my favorite color."

Calvin closed his eyes and pinched the bridge of his nose, saying, "Junior, the color don't matter. What *does* matter is I can get in and hot-wire the damn thing. I don't like messin' with no foreign cars, only American. They're easier. *Got it?*"

"Yeah, yeah, sure Calvin. Whatever you say." Junior sniffed and scraped something out of his eye, jerking his head around to see what was behind him, then looked at Calvin. "Hey man, lemme have just a little bit, just a little." Holding his thumb and finger up about an inch apart.

"No. How many times I gotta tell you? I need you thinkin' straight. You get any of that stuff in you and you ain't for nothin'."

"Yeah, I know, man, it's just that"—looking around the parking lot like he was searching for snipers—"a little bit will like, smooth me out. Ya know?"

Calvin blinked once, keeping a straight face, and held back the urge to backhand his friend one good time like he'd seen DeNiro do in the movies. "No, once we done the job and split the money up, you can have some. Not till then."

"But I—" Calvin's look shut him up.

They walked through the Olive Garden parking lot all the way to the far end before they found what they were looking for.

"That one," Calvin said, stopping and nodding. "The Chrysler 300."

"The red car?"

"It's not red. It's like a maroon or burgundy or maybe one of them new colors, like cinnamon or something."

"Looks red to me."

Calvin cocked his head to the side and squinted at Junior. He kept his lips tight and said nothing, let the silence speak for itself. Junior peered down at his feet and shuffled them around. He sucked in his top lip and bit it, waiting for Calvin to stop looking at him like that.

Calvin walked over to the car.

Five seconds; that's all it took for Calvin to pop the lock. Fifteen more and he had it started, some Amy Grant crap coming out of the speakers. Junior sat there with his mouth open, watching Calvin do his thing when he should have been watching for the owners coming out of the restaurant.

Calvin turned to Junior and flashed a smile, the kind that said lookie-what-I-can-do, then scrunched his face up as he saw two people running toward them: a hot looking chick in tight jeans and a dude in a suit. Calvin said, "Oh shit!" then shifted into reverse, stomped on the gas, backed out and slammed on the brakes, shifted into drive and squealed out of the parking lot.

"They looked pissed," Junior said through a laugh as they sped down the road.

"You were supposed to be watching out."

"I was."

"No, you weren't. You were watching *me*."

Junior was quiet for a second. "We made it."

Calvin looked at Junior, then looked ahead, leaving it at that.

A couple of minutes later, Junior said, "Where we goin'?"

"Home."

"I thought we's gonna—"

"Not till it's dark."

"Dark? I can't wait till it's dark." Junior's eyes grew bigger than moonpies. "I need somethin' *right now*."

"Sorry, man. Gotta wait till dark." Calvin looked at Junior sitting forward in his seat, biting his fingernails, bags under his eyes. "Sorry," he repeated. "You know how you get."

At home, Junior paced continuously, wearing a track in the carpet around the coffee table as big as Martinsville Speedway. Calvin started to yell out to him about Gordon and Petty coming up on the outside but thought then that it might freak him out more. Junior was pretty geeked up as it was. Calvin wanted to give him a little something but once he did, Junior'd not have any incentive to do the job. Plus, he needed Junior as sharp as he could possibly be and that wasn't much to begin with.

Maybe Junior could have a little piece, Calvin thought, just enough to smooth him out like he said earlier, take the edge off, calm him down a tad. Just a little. Calvin went back to his bedroom, pulled a twenty-rock out of the bureau drawer where it was stuffed in a pair of black socks in the back, cut it in two with his pocketknife and returned half to the drawer. He went back to the living room and gave it to Junior, holding it out in his hand without saying a word, watching Junior's face come alive as he figured out what it was, not at all disappointed that it was small.

Calvin went to make a stiff drink while Junior pulled out his pipe and fired it up. Calvin preferred straight vodka to anything. He could still think and drive on vodka; hell, he thought he drove better after a drink or two. Made him pay more attention.

Calvin returned to a cloudy living room. Junior was laying on the couch, eyes half closed, a stupid smile on his face like one of those guys in the crazy house that's always drooling on himself. Calvin flipped on the TV, looking for something to kill time till dark, thinking they probably shouldn't have stolen the car until dark so they could have gone straight out and done the job instead of doing all this sitting around and waiting first.

He found an old rerun of Andy Griffith on TV, the episode where Opie gets a pocketknife from Mister MacBeavey and Andy thinks Opie made the guy up 'cause Opie says MacBeavey walks in the trees and jingles. Andy's about ready to tan his hide for lying when he walks out to the woods where Opie says the guy is, shouts the guy's name in frustration, and then the guy climbs down from a tree, jingling and everything 'cause as it turns out, he's a telephone repairman.

A commercial came on selling a revolutionary new nose hair trimmer and Junior said, "Man, I gotta get one of them." He watched the guy on the TV stick it up his nose and twirl it around, smiling like trimming his nose hair was fun.

Calvin looked at Junior and said, "I got one."

"You got one?"

Calvin said yeah, he had one.

"That same one?"

Calvin watched the commercial for a second. "Not that exact one, but I got one. Mine's longer and thinner with a black case."

"Lemme see."

Calvin looked over at Junior a second, studying him, and said, "Why?"

"Cause I wanna see it."

"It looks almost like that one." He pointed to the TV but the commercial had already gone off, an ad for life insurance on now with that Ed McMahon guy that used to do the commercials where they surprised people with a couple million bucks. The guy made you feel like anyone could just wake up one day and find a bunch of money.

"So you not gonna let me see it?"

"You wanna see it that bad? It's in the bathroom, under the sink."

Junior pulled himself up while Calvin said, "I don't see what the big deal is; it's a fuckin' nose hair trimmer." He watched Junior teeter down the hall and into the bathroom, still reeling from the effects of that hit an hour before.

"Hey!" Calvin yelled out when he heard the humming noise. "What the fuck you doin'? Hey! I said what the fuck you doin'?"

The noise stopped and Junior said, "I was just seeing how it worked."

"You ain't fuckin' *using* it are you? You better not be using it!"

Junior stumbled back into the hall, saying, "Relax, man, I was just testing it out, just turning it on to see how it worked."

"Yeah, well, you better not have used it or I'd have to kick your fuckin' ass."

* * *

CALVIN SHOOK JUNIOR and said, "Come on, man.  It's time, let's go do this."  Junior opened his eyes from his nap, looking around like he didn't know where he was at.  He sat up and held onto the side of the couch, shaking his head to wake completely up.

"You ready?"  Calvin said.

Junior nodded with his eyes still not all the way open, smacking his lips like they were dry.

Before they got to the car, Junior got the jitters, saying, "Lemme have another hit, man, just a small one, like what you gave me earlier.  I need it, dude."

"No, we gonna do this and I need you alert, man.  I told you this already, so get it in your fuckin' head that you ain't gettin' any more till we score."

Calvin slid behind the wheel and started the car even quicker than before.  Junior hopped in the passenger seat and fidgeted around like he had bees crawling all over him.

They drove for awhile, Junior saying every few miles, "How about that one?"  Pointing out the window.  Calvin answered, "Nope," every time.  Junior just wanted to hit something quick without scouting anything out first.

On the other side of town, Calvin pulled into the parking lot of a convenience store.  He flipped the light on inside the car and looked at Junior.  "Okay, this is the one."

"This one?"  Junior jerked his head to look out the window.

"Yeah, see the clerk?  She's a little older and don't look like she's gonna cause no trouble.  And there's only a few people in there.  They'll leave in a few minutes and that's when you'll hit it."

Junior calmed for a second and turned back to Calvin, letting it sink in. Then his eyes got big and he said, "Me?"

"Yeah, you."

"Why me?"  Junior rubbed his nose hard.

"Cause I'm a foreman at Kohler Construction and you're just a Walmart greeter."

"What's that got to do with anything?  You know I cain't walk right."

"You got a gun, you can walk any way you want."

Junior scrunched his face together and paused, then said, "But I thought we was doin' it together."

"We are.  Somebody's gotta keep the getaway car runnin'."

"I can drive!"

Calvin looked at Junior like he'd just cussed his mother.  "No, you can't.  I ain't letting you drive with you like that."

"Like what?"

"All nervous and shit."

"I ain't nervous." Junior's eyes blinked, one right after another like they forgot to blink at the same time.

"Plus, we only got one gun so what's the other guy gonna do, make mean faces at everybody?"  Junior didn't say a word and Calvin continued, "And besides, I'm the one—*what the fuck?*  You used my nose hair trimmer didn't you, asshole?"

Junior looked away and sniffed, saying, "No, I told you I only turned the thing on to see what it was like."

"Bullshit, look at me.  Look at me *goddammit*."  Junior turned his head slowly until he was facing Calvin.  "You little motherfucker, you *did* use it! You only got one of your fuckin' nostrils."

Junior brought his hand up to his nose, playing with it, scratching it.

Calvin said, "Goddam, I can't believe you.  You put my nose hair trimmer up your fuckin' nose; now I gotta throw it away and get another." Calvin shook his head, he couldn't believe it. "You wipe your ass with my toothbrush too?"

Junior still kept quiet, looking at all the lights on the dashboard, finding something interesting enough in them not to look Calvin in the eyes.

Then Calvin burst out laughing, saying, "I just remembered something. Last time I used it, last Saturday, I cut my pubes.  Spent fifteen minutes down there gettin' it all nice and pretty for Angela cause she won't go down on me if it's a jungle."

Junior wiped his nose like he'd just snorted a whole kilo of powder, like a group of mosquitoes had flown up there and he was trying to get them out. Calvin watched him and laughed, thinking it was the best revenge he could have hoped for.  He added, "So you've had something up your nose that's been on my pecker.  I'm gonna start callin' you Peckernose."  Laughing till he almost peed his pants, picturing Junior's nose as a big pecker.

A pair of girls left the store and a man in a business suit entered.

"*Damn*.  This place is too busy.  We're gonna have to find somewhere else," Calvin said, looking at the store and the people milling around inside, gripping the gearshift tight.

"No, let's not drive around no more."  Junior's face jerked from the store to Calvin.  "I'll do it, I can do it.  Gimme the gun."  Holding his hand out, trying to keep it from shaking.

"You sure you ready, man?"

"Yeah, yeah.  Just gimme the gun and let me get it over with."

Calvin looked at him, studying him, wondering if he was okay enough to do this, thinking he should have probably given Junior another little hit to smooth him out like he wanted. Probably. "Alright, look ... be cool in there, okay?"

"Yeah, whatever." Junior held out his hand and wiggled his fingers.

Calvin gave him the gun and watched him get out of the car, look around the parking lot and back behind him, then walk up to the door, throw it open and run inside waving the gun around yelling at everybody.

Calvin watched from the car as Junior belted commands to the woman behind the counter. She opened the register and filled a paper bag with money. Everything was going perfect, just like it was supposed to, till Junior started talking to some redneck in line. Junior then looked inside the paper bag, got upset and said something. The redneck talked to him, not even flinching when Junior pointed the gun at him.

The clerk opened the register again and put some more bills into the bag. Then Junior stood there talking to the redneck again, for a long time. Then ... *what the hell?* Junior gave the paper bag back to the clerk, backed out of the store and ran across the parking lot to the car.

He opened the passenger door and got in, eyes bugging out, gun shoved in his pants, sweat beading on his forehead like it was a hundred percent humidity outside. Junior looked straight ahead, a tic bothering his left eye, saying, "Let's go."

Calvin stared at him. "What the hell happened in there?"

"Just go, man."

"But you didn't get nothing."

"Let's go! We'll hit another place."

"But I already picked out *this* place. What happened in there?"

Junior finally turned to Calvin, his eyes looking like that crazy guy in the old Disney movies, like at any moment they were going to pop out in his lap. "Nothing happened, that's what happened, *nothing*! Now come on, man, let's go!"

Calvin squealed his tires and spun out of the parking lot, took off down the road at twice the speed limit, then slowed down so they didn't attract attention. Calvin asked again, "Okay, what the fuck happened back there?"

"I'll tell you later, man. *Alright?* That cool?"

"Yeah, sure, but—"

"*Stop!* Pull in over here, yeah, right here." Calvin yanked the car into another convenience store parking lot, over to the side, not right up in front of the door where there was a place open.

Calvin said, "Okay man, you gonna—" But Junior was already out the car, pulling the gun out of his pants, striding with purpose toward the side door of the place.

Calvin watched as Junior ran in like he did at the other place, yelling and waving his gun at everybody. The clerk reached under the counter and pulled out a shotgun. Junior shouted and jerked his shooting hand back and forth. Then the clerk leveled the shotgun right at Junior's chest and pulled the trigger. Junior flew backwards, coming off his feet just like in the movies, crashing into a display of chips, squashing them underneath him as he landed on his back. He didn't move.

Calvin waited a second to see if Junior was going to get up, then punched the gas down to the floor. He careened off a big Lincoln, jumped the curb and flew down the street, his tires barely touching the pavement. His heart pumped wildly and his hands shook like he had some old man's disease. He couldn't believe Junior was dead and gone. He felt faint as the image of Junior's blood flying everywhere replayed in his mind.

The Chrysler screamed down the street and it was a couple of blocks before Calvin looked up in his rearview and saw the blue lights flashing, hearing the *wahhhh* as the siren started up.  Calvin's brain began running as fast as the Chrysler he was in.

He started thinking, remembering back, guessing there was nothing to tie him to Junior going in that store 'cause nobody had seen him in the car. Probably.

Calvin pulled over into the parking lot of an out-of-business dry cleaner and stopped over a yellow line on the pavement, pushing a button on the door and rolling his window down.

The cop car pulled in and stopped behind him, the lights still blinking but the siren off.  It sat there, motionless, the cop inside doing something on his dashboard, probably running the plate.  Then Calvin remembered that he wasn't in *his* car, he was in one he and Junior had stolen just to go and rob a convenience store.

Oh shit, thinking to himself, he was going to get busted for boosting the car.  But at least he wasn't going to go down for the armed robbery.  He could deny anything to do with all that, *hell*, even a court-appointed lawyer could get him out of it.  Maybe even get the stolen car thing knocked down to joyriding or some other misdemeanor bullshit, get out with probation or community service.  Maybe just a hundred dollar fine and a promise to be a good boy and stop acting like a teenager.

The cop stepped out of his car and adjusted the hat on his head, twisting his belt around a little, reminding Calvin of Barney Fife every time he pulled someone over.  Except this cop was short and stocky.  The cop shifted his piece into just the right spot and came up on the driver's side real slow, keeping one hand on his holster, the other holding a big black flashlight that he was moving back and forth over the car, shining it in the back seat as he walked up beside him, then pointing it at Calvin's lap. "License and registration."

Calvin, still sort of stunned, took a moment to react.  He reached over and pushed the glove box button, let the door pop down, and pulled out an envelope.  After rifling through it, he pulled out a little piece of paper and handed it to the cop with his license.  He read the cop's nametag.  *F. Faustino.*

The cop took the license, saying, "Is this your car, sir?"

Calvin thought, what the hell, let's play it out.  "Uh, no sir.  It's a friend's, Mr. Faustino."

"*Officer* Faustino."  The cop pointed the flashlight at him, then at the registration, then back at him.  "This Sarah Nealey your friend?"

"Yeah, yeah … she's my girlfriend, *Officer* Faustino."  Calvin wondered where the hell that came from.  He was concentrating so hard on getting the cop's name right, he just answered.

"Your girlfriend?"

"Yeah." *Shit.*

"Then why didn't you say that at first?  That she was your girlfriend?  You said the car was your friend's, not your girlfriend's."

*Fuck.*  "Well, we were friends before we dated."  Crossing his fingers in his head.

The cop was silent for a second, still pointing the flashlight at Calvin's chest.  "Have you been drinking tonight, sir?"  The cop nodded.  "I'm willing to bet you have."

"Uh … yeah, sorta … I had some vodka earlier."  Then adding quick, "A coupla hours ago."

"With your girlfriend?"

"Yeah, with my girlfriend."

"Where is she now, sir?"

Calvin's brain was starting to hurt now.  "Back at the house."

"Her house or yours?"

"Hers."

"Her house in ... " The cop looked at the registration. "Minnesota?"

"Minne ...?" *Shit, shit, shit!* "Oh, no, her house here. She must not have gotten her registration changed since she moved." Calvin was thinking fast now, forgetting to say the Officer Faustino part.

The cop looked at him for a moment before saying he'd be right back, then walked to his car and slid into the driver's seat. He fiddled around the dashboard for a bit, then got out and returned to the spot he was before, just outside Calvin's door.

"Mister Watkins? Do you have any idea how fast you were going back there?"

"Uh, no sir. Thirty?"

Officer Faustino looked at him. "Were you in a hurry to get somewhere?"

Calvin thought that it was the opposite, he was in a hurry to get *away* from somewhere. He said, "No, sir. I was just ... being stupid. Gunnin' it to see how she handled." He winked and patted the steering wheel.

The cop nodded and smiled, then said, "Sir, I'm gonna need you to step out of the car."

"What's wrong?"

"Sir, will you just step out of the car, please?" His voice was a little harder now than the first time he asked and he fingered the grip on his gun like it was itching him.

Calvin thought for a split second he could shift into gear and take off but it was too late, the cop already had his ID. So he opened the door and stepped out while the cop backed up, that one hand of his still playing with the handle of his gun, the other keeping the flashlight trained on him.

The cop, at least six inches shorter than Calvin, motioned for Calvin to turn around. "Put your hands on top of the car and spread your legs. A little more. That's good. You're not carrying any weapons are you?" he said as he began patting Calvin down.

"No, no weapons."

"Okay, sir." The cop finished up. "Do you mind if I have a look inside your girlfriend's car?"

"Uh … no, no problem."

The cop told him to stand at the front of the car, his hands on the hood, and not to move while he looked around. Calvin stood there, leaning over, watching the cop root around the front seats, move to the back seats, then get out and come up to him with something in his hands. "Mister Watkins, what is this?"

He held up a little baggie with some dried herbs inside, Calvin guessing it probably wasn't oregano. "I don't know, it's not mine." Calvin wasn't believing his luck, that the one car he chose to steal had a bag of pot and now he was going to wear the charge for it.

"I see; it's your girlfriend's then?"

Calvin weighed his options, wondering if admitting the car was stolen was a good thing or not but then thinking that a stolen car might pull more time or something, saying, "Yeah, that's it, it's hers. I mean, this is her car, you know?"

"And you're sure it's not your stash?"

"Yeah, I didn't even know it was in the car, I swear." He started to hold up his hands like a Boy Scout but then thought better about any sudden movements.

"Uh-huh. Are you a betting man, Mr. Watkins?" Officer Faustino said.

"Huh? Betting?"

"Yeah, cause I'm a betting man … and I'm willing to bet this here baggie is yours, not your girlfriend's." Officer Faustino pointed his square jaw at Calvin. "You mind if I check in the trunk?"

"Uh … yeah, sure … go right ahead. I got nothing to hide, officer."

The cop motioned and Calvin reached in the front and pushed the trunk button. The cop said he was going to have to cuff him, told him to put his hands behind his back and slapped the cuffs on them. Then the cop walked to the back of the car, keeping an eye on Calvin, looked inside the trunk for a second, checked on Calvin again, leaned in, then slid his head out the side to look at Calvin. Calvin just stood there with his hands cuffed behind him.

The cop came back to the front holding a big shopping bag in his hand, looking at Calvin with a blank expression. "Mr. Watkins, do you know what was back there in your girlfriend's trunk?"

Calvin shook his head hard, saying fast, "Whatever it is, it's not mine. I swear. It's not mine. I didn't have nothing to do with it." What had the cop found? *A meth lab? A shipment of coke? A couple bricks of heroine?*

"You sure? It's not yours?"

"Yeah, I'm pretty sure. I don't got a clue what was in that trunk."

"*Pretty* sure? Or *definitely* sure?"

Calvin had to pee now. "*Definitely* sure. Absolutely *definitely* sure."

"Yeah, I'm betting you're definitely sure." The cop held the bag out, opening it so Calvin could look inside, and said, "There's probably a couple million bucks in here. Think carefully about your answer cause that decides where we go from here. Do you understand?"

Calvin nodded his head slowly, his eyes locked on all the stacks of hundreds in the bag.

"So, again, I'll ask you. Is this yours?"

Calvin frowned and looked up. "What if it was only partly mine, if you know what I'm saying?" Calvin raised his eyebrows.

The cop returned his gaze with a straight face, still holding the bag open, and said, "What if I pulled you over for speeding and you got a bullet in you for trying to take my gun?"

Calvin's stomach soured as he looked from Officer F. Faustino to the cash and back up, his mind going blank except for one thought, how the night would have gone different if only he'd given Junior a loaded gun.

97

"If I can't get the girl, at least give me more money"

*Alan Alda*

# #5

# Everybody's Got A Magic Number

"WHAT'S THE LINE on the game this weekend?" Mikey B. said, leaning with his elbows on the kitchen counter. He chewed on a toothpick and had his Chicago Bulls cap on sideways.

"Which game?" Timmy Ray asked. He sat at the breakfast table, his foot propped up on another chair, fingers busy with shoelaces. He strained to reach over his potbelly, never once seeing his shoes, having to tie them by feel alone.

"Which game? Whaddya mean which game? *The* game: Carolina at Duke." Mikey B. pushed up off the counter and grabbed a green apple from Timmy Ray's fruit bowl, fiddling around with it while he was talking. "So what's the line on it?"

Timmy Ray dropped his foot to the floor with a huff, glad to have the pressure off his mid-section, and straightened his shirt over his belly like he was a private in the Army.  "Well, I was thinkin' about givin' five points to Duke."

"Five points?  To Duke?  But it's *at* Duke!"

Timmy Ray shrugged as he stood and pulled his pants up by his belt, then patted his pockets to make sure everything was there.  "So?  Duke sucks this year.  I think Coach K's losin' his touch.  Maybe he should step down, let Amaker take over before they lose him to another program. Anyways, I figure with this line, most people'll take Duke and I'll rack up."

"Whatever," Mikey B. said, turning the apple over in his hands.  "It's not like you need the money anyway."

"That's not the point.  You think I do this for the money?"  Timmy Ray threw his hands up.  "I do it cause I'm bored and I like parting suckers from their wallets."

"Well, I guess you know what you're doing," Mikey B. said as he took a bite out of the apple he'd been fondling.

"You *damn straight* I know what I'm doing," Timmy Ray said, watching Mikey B. spit the apple piece out into his hand, a grimace plastered over his face.  "What the hell?" Timmy Ray asked.

"Ugh, man.  This apple's sour."  Mikey B.'s face contorted like he'd just walked into the bathroom after one of Timmy Ray's famous dumps, the kind he bragged would not only peel the paint but also melt the putty out of the cracks in the drywall.

"It's a Granny Smith."

"So?"  Mikey B. said, scraping his tongue with his teeth, spitting all the pieces he could find out into his hand, then looking at them like doing that would make the taste go away.

"So, don't you know anything?  Granny Smiths are *supposed* to be sour. That's why you buy 'em."  Timmy Ray pulled his keys out of his pocket and played with them as he talked.

"Why would anyone want to eat a sour apple?"

"*Why would* ...?" Timmy Ray looked at Mikey B. like it was the first time he'd ever met him, not believing Mikey B. didn't know about sour apples, not understanding how he could be that stupid. Then shaking his head, Timmy Ray said, "Look, we gotta go. Tee time's in thirty minutes."

"Who we playin' with today?"

"Nunya."

"Nunya?"

Timmy Ray wondered just how many branches Mikey B. hit when he fell from the stupid tree. He cracked a smile as he said, "Nunya damn business." Then he motioned toward the door while saying, "Come on, we gotta go."

* * *

"YOU CAN'T WEAR that hat out here," Timmy Ray said as he pulled his clubs out of the back of his Lincoln Navigator, popped the stand out, and set it on the pavement.

"What's wrong with my hat?" Mikey B. said as he fingered the bill over his left ear.

"What's wrong with it? It's not appropriate wear for a golf course; that's what's wrong with it. It's a friggin' Chicago Bulls cap, for Christ's sake."

"So?"

Timmy Ray sighed, seeing he wasn't going to win this one, realizing he was going to have to pick his battles. Mikey B. didn't like to be without a hat 'cause he was going bald as a baby's ass. "Well at least turn it around like a white boy."

"Aw, come on man. Why you gotta be like that?"

"I'm serious about this, man, I ain't going on the course with you wearing your cap sideways like that. It just ain't happenin'." Timmy Ray closed the back of his Navigator and stood there, raising his eyebrows at Mikey B., neither of them moving. After ten seconds, Mikey B. finally rolled his eyes and turned his cap so the bill pointed forward.

They met up with Dwayne Crawford and Joey Pierce in the pro shop. Mikey B. knew them both; they all went way back, even before Mikey B. dated Joey's younger sister, Joanne. He was going to take her to the prom junior year but she told him she wasn't giving him her cherry like she'd promised; so instead, he went with Dena Coble, left the prom early, and screwed for two hours straight in the hotel room he booked a month earlier, when he was still planning on taking Joanne. It would have been worth it if Dena hadn't given him that rash that didn't go away for a month.

Timmy Ray said, "Let's get a few drinks in the clubhouse before we head out on the course."

Dwayne said, "Nah, I got a cooler of cold ones in my truck, we'll stop by with the carts on the way to number one and grab 'em. I ain't paying no two bucks for a damn beer. That's fuckin' robbery, man."

At the first hole, they began their rituals. Joey slid a donut weight onto his driver and swung it back and forth like he was Chi Chi Rodriguez, wearing the same kind of hat Chi Chi did. He only wore it when he played golf, thinking it helped his game. Dwayne did his stretches, holding his club over his head with both hands, then bending over at the waist, keeping his legs straight as he could, bringing the club all the way to his ankles, then back up over his head again. Mikey B. warmed-up by drinking two of the beers from Dwayne's cooler, one right after another with barely enough time to suck some oxygen in between them.

Timmy Ray waddled up to the tee box, got down on one knee, shoved the ball and tee into the grass, and almost fell over as he got back up. Then he took a few practice swings that people told him looked like he was in one of them fake sumo wrestler costumes.  That was his warm-up; he never actually got warm.

They decided to play skins:  Timmy Ray and Mikey B. against Dwayne and Joey, a hundred bucks a hole.  Timmy Ray, on the tee box, turned and said, "Birdies, greenies and sandies count?"

Dwayne looked up from his stretches, nodding, and said, "Eagles count two."  He twisted at his waist, still stretching and looking like that curly-headed queer that sold the Oldies workout tapes his ex-wife always bought when they were still together.  She only used them a couple times, Dwayne said once, so her ass was still the size of Montana.

"Yeah, right," Timmy Ray said.  "Dwayne, you couldn't hit an eagle if it bit your nuts."  Mikey B. and Joey chuckled.

"Yeah?  We'll see about that, *Fatty Ray*.  You just be sure and have your wallet ready when the day's over."

"Fatty Ray?  That the best you can do, Dwayne?  I tell you what, I'd rather be fat than ugly.  I can always lose weight, but man, you're fucked your whole life."  He got more laughs from Mikey B. and Joey.  Dwayne's face reddened as he blurted out to just hit the damn ball or he'd come up there and hit it himself.

So Timmy Ray did, turning and squaring up beside it, yanking his brand new Callaway driver back like it had bugs crawling on it, then swinging it around hard and smacking the ball right on the Titleist logo. The ball flew straight and long with a little draw on it, ending up about two fifty down the middle of the fairway, just outside a nasty bunker to the left. Timmy Ray hobbled down off the tee box, sporting a shit-eating grin, and shoved his club into his bag.  He whistled through his teeth as he squeezed in behind the steering wheel on his cart and popped the top on a beer.

Mikey B. steadied himself, swung, and topped the ball, knocking it about a hundred yards. He threw his driver half that distance, yelling, "Fuck-mother-goddam-fuck!"

Joey said, "Maybe you shoulda had another beer for warm-ups." Mikey B. glared at him as he returned to the cart.

Dwayne was next. He took his time with a couple of practice swings, then studied the course and checked the wind with a wet finger. He stepped up to the ball, waggled his hips, shook his arms, bounced up and down, and finally cocked his head, looking out toward the green.

Timmy Ray said, "You gonna hit the ball or take it on a date and fuck it first?" The guys chuckled, Timmy Ray knowing it would get under Dwayne's skin.

It worked. Dwayne backed off the ball, turned around and told Timmy Ray, "Why don't you come up here and suck my hairy dick." He grabbed his crotch with his gloved hand and squeezed. Everybody laughed, even Timmy Ray, and the damage was done.

Dwayne shanked the ball, barely nicking it and sending it diagonal into the woods to the right. He yelled, "Fucking cocksucker!" Then slammed his club down into the tee box so hard it made an impression in the ground.

Joey came up behind him, saying, "Don't let him get to you, Dwayne. He does the same shit every time and you always let it get to you."

No one said anything to Joey 'cause nothing much really affected his game. Timmy Ray had tried everything, from talking about his mother, to picking on him about his smooth legs, to ripping a loud one during his backswing. Nothing ever fazed Joey; he popped the ball down the middle a little over two hundred yards out, just like he always did.

By the sixth hole, they were tied three-all with no carry-overs and no extras. Nobody had hit the green on the par three at number four, despite it being a hundred fifty with no traps or water. Nobody scored a sandie out of a bunker.  And the closest anybody got to hitting a birdie or an eagle was when Mikey B. just missed killing a fat goose on hole number two when he sliced into the lake on his first shot.  Goose didn't even flinch, water spraying on it like in a movie.

They finished Dwayne's beer by the time they came around to the clubhouse after number nine, Timmy Ray and Mikey B. up in skins, five to four.  They all took a piss, grabbed a hot dog and one of them two-dollar beers and met at the tee box on hole number ten.

Timmy Ray ran his mouth, saying how they were going to whip Dwayne's and Joey's asses on the back nine.  Mikey B. didn't say a word 'cause he shot a fifty-two on the front, Timmy Ray having to carry their team as usual.

"Oh yeah?  Well, why don't you put your money where your fat mouth is?" Dwayne finally blurted out, his face as red as the Chicago Bulls logo on Mikey B.'s ball cap.

"What you sayin', Dwayne?"

"What'm I sayin'?  Hundred a hole is for pussies, is what I'm sayin'.  How about a grand a hole?  For the whole eighteen, so you already got a thousand in your pocket as a cushion."  Then added, "Like you need more cushion in there."

Timmy Ray cocked his eyebrows and popped the top on his two-dollar beer, not believing what he just heard from Dwayne.  Didn't even care he threw in a fat joke.  What it was:  a grand a hole was still pussy money to Timmy Ray (sometimes he liked to say God came to *him* for loans); but to Dwayne, a grand a hole was big.  Real big.

Mikey B. whistled and turned his cap back sideways like he always wore it, looking from Timmy Ray to Dwayne and back to Timmy Ray.

"You sure you can handle that, Dwayne?"  Timmy Ray said after a moment, still sitting in his seat, looking over at Dwayne who was standing on the cart path in front of him, gripping a fag-yellow Top-Flite ball in his gloved hand.  Timmy Ray always made fun of Dwayne and his neon fag-colored balls, yellow and orange and pink, like he was playing at a Putt-Putt or something.  Timmy Ray was a golf elitist of sorts, preferring only straight white golf balls, *cause that's the way God made 'em.*

"I can handle it, can you?" Dwayne said, a scowl on his face.

Before he could answer, the beer cart pulled up.  Driving it was a ripe young slice of American pie, a vision right out of Playboy's ACC campus review wearing tightly-woven pigtails and an even tighter lime green t-shirt that read "Kiss my Irish half."

Timmy Ray immediately squeezed out of the cart and approached the girl with a king-size grin on his face.  Mikey B. followed right behind him, smiling so big his one gold tooth gleamed in the midday sun like the hood ornament on an old Buick.

"Well hello darlin', where you been all my life?" Timmy Ray said as he waddled close, watching every inch of her as she rose from her seat.  She stood a full two inches taller than him and wore a pair of painted-on cream shorts and white tennis shoes with no socks.  Her long legs were bronzed to perfection.

"At Wake Forest," she said as she opened one of her coolers, bending at the waist slightly, leaning over just enough to stop the breath of every male within a hundred yards.

"College girl, huh?" Timmy Ray said, checking out her assets.  "This your regular job?"

"I fill in for Tami sometimes."  She pulled out a tray filled with peanut butter crackers and candy bars.  "You guys see anything you like?"  She flashed a steady smile, her blue eyes clear and playful.

By now, the four golfers had surrounded her, each experiencing naughty thoughts, forgetting they were all at least ten years her senior, not caring about it either.

"Which is your Irish half?" Mikey B. said, hooking his thumbs into the waistband of his pants, his hat still sideways, keeping his smile big enough so she'd see his gold tooth.

The girl looked him square in the face, saying, "Well, my dad's the Irish one and he's a total ass so *you* figure it out." She looked at him without blinking, smiling when all the other guys said a collective *oooh*.

Joey punched Mikey B. in the arm saying something about being shot down before he even got off the runway.

"Nasty mouth on such a pretty little thing," Timmy Ray said with a laugh.

She said back, "It's a whole lot nastier than *you'll* ever know." Everybody laughed except Timmy Ray whose mouth opened slightly like he forgot what he was going to say next.

"Don't worry about Timmy Ray here," Dwayne jumped in, "he suffers from *dickey-dew* disease."

"*Dickey-dew* disease?" she said.

"Yeah, it's been ten years since he seen below his waist so he don't know what his dickey do no more." Dwayne guffawed, laughing louder than he should have, slapping his knee, eventually stopping when he saw nobody was enjoying the joke as much as him.

"Geez, Dwayne," Timmy Ray said, looking at him like he'd just shown everyone the hairy mole on his ass. Then looking at the girl, he said, "You gotta excuse our friend. He don't get out in public much on account of all them botched penile implant operations. It was only three inches when he went for the first one"—holding up a golf pencil—"and now it's up to five but it's still only as big around as this thing." He waved the pencil around while everybody but Dwayne laughed, the girl rolling her eyes and smiling.

Timmy Ray kept on going. "It's so small around that on his wedding night, his wife kept asking him if it was in yet." Timmy Ray reveled in the laughter that followed, Dwayne's face reddening so much that Timmy Ray thought he'd melt his bushy mustache off. "Matter of fact, he came in one time and found her gang-banging a box of Crayolas." Everybody but Dwayne laughed again.

The girl finally said, "Alright, you guys, save it for the golf course. I've got other customers to get to. Anybody want anything?"

Timmy Ray was on a roll now, saying, "What can I get for a twenty?" Wiggling his eyebrows, holding out a crisp new bill creased down the middle longways.

The girl didn't flinch, coming back with, "About forty Snickers and type two diabetes. Or ten beers and a nasty hangover. Your choice." Standing there with one hand on her hip, the other holding the tray of snacks.

It was Timmy Ray's turn to be laughed at, poked in the arm and chastised like the fat pimply kid in gym class who couldn't do a pull-up.

He countered with, "I tell you what, honey, you finish out the last nine holes with us, I'll give you five of these bills. That's a hundred bucks for the next two hours; whatcha say?" He reached in his pocket and pulled out his money clip, peeling four crisp new bills off and creasing them longways just like the first one.

She squinted her eyes and looked at him, saying, "And all I gotta do is follow you guys till you finish your game? No funny business?"

Timmy Ray smiled, seeing he had her now. One thing he knew about in this world was the power of money. He knew how money worked and more importantly, he knew how to make it work for him.

Timmy Ray always got what he wanted, partly because he always had the money to get it, and partly because he never stopped until he got it.  And once that beer cart had pulled up, he'd had only one thing on his mind.

He said, "You got it.  You just follow us around, sell us food and beer when we want it, hang out with us, and you get a hundred dollar tip."  Then Timmy Ray winked and said, "Any funny business is extra."  Before she could answer, he grabbed a new ball from his bag and walked up on the tee box with his driver.

By the end of the hole, they learned her name was Caroline and she was third year pre-med, leaning toward being a pediatrician.  Twice she fended off jokes about how much she'd charge for a prostate exam.

Dwayne and Joey won two skins when Joey chipped in a birdie from just below the green.  Both of them jumped up and down when it happened, then froze and watched open-mouthed as Caroline jumped up and down, clapping, her big boobs bouncing in opposite rhythm from her body.  Timmy Ray thought she was going to give herself a black eye if she kept it up.

Dwayne and Joey won the next hole, too, it being a long par five with a dog-leg right.  Joey drove long down the left side, getting lucky when it hit the cart path and picked up another sixty yards past everyone else, then hit over the woods on the corner with a high five-iron, and chucked a sweet nine-iron up to the green and two-putted for par.  Timmy Ray and Mikey B, trying to show off for Caroline, attempted the same second shot over the woods but they came up short, each of them eventually finishing with an eight.

The twelfth hole, a short par three over water with woods close on both sides, didn't go much better than the eleventh.  Timmy Ray dropped it in the drink just five feet short of the shore and he depended on Mikey B. to win, which, after Mikey B. stuck the green on his tee shot, he thought might happen. Maybe even get a greenie and a birdie, go up by one in the skins. But Mikey B. three-putted, amazingly, missing a little one-footer by leaving it short. Dwayne and Joey gave him hell, asking him if his husband played and was his skirt too tight.

Suddenly, Timmy Ray was down three thousand dollars and the game got serious. For him anyway. They were winning until Caroline joined them and he realized that he and Mikey B. had been distracted, while Dwayne and Joey weren't. That was the opposite of what he'd hoped. So he had an idea, a way to turn the tables.

Pulling Caroline to the side, he told her something that made her shake her head, then told her something else. He nodded and made some gestures, still talking, then nodded some more and waited. She finally nodded and smiled back.

Timmy Ray wedged himself behind the wheel of his cart and Mikey B. asked, "What was that all about?"

Timmy Ray hit the gas pedal and the golf cart hummed, picking up speed. "Things are about to get a lot more interesting." Then looking Mikey B. in the face, he said, "I need you to keep your mind on the game and not the girl."

"What? Why?"

Timmy Ray smiled, looking forward again. "Let's just say I've given her an incentive for us to win our bet."

"Like what?"

"Don't you worry about it. You just focus on hittin' that little white ball in the hole."

Just before Dwayne teed off on the thirteenth, Caroline's voice drifted over to them. "Hey, you guys don't mind if I take this off do you?" When everyone looked, she was holding up a lacy bra, the cups bigger than

Timmy Ray's fat head.  Then she ran her hands over her chest, saying how that felt so much better now and why didn't she think of that sooner.

Dwayne shanked his shot far right; in fact, it was so far right it flew over the next fairway and into the same pond where Mikey B. almost killed the goose earlier.  Joey's swing dug into the tee box, hitting the ball almost as an afterthought, sending it just shy of the ladie's tee, a whole fifty yards ahead.

Timmy Ray howled, pumping his fist, while Mikey B. taunted Joey, telling him, "Now you gotta drop your drawers."

Timmy Ray and Mikey B. each knocked their shots out in the fairway, Timmy Ray's about another twenty yards further than Mikey B's.  When Joey went to hit his second shot, Mikey B. reminded him, "Don't forget to drop 'em."

"But—" Joey said, looking back at the girl.  She sat in her cart, her legs propped up on the dash, looking like she was posing for a magazine.

"Oh no, that makes no difference," Mikey B. said, "Whether she's here or not, you still gotta follow the rules."

"What's the deal, fellas?" Caroline finally asked, scratching her side where the bra had dug into her skin.

Timmy Ray spoke up, "See, we gotta rule.  You don't hit it past the ladie's tee, you gotta drop your pants to hit the next shot."

"That's sexist," she said.

Timmy Ray shrugged, saying, "Yeah, so?  We're pigs, sue us.  But it's the rules."  Then he looked over at Joey standing at his ball, holding a three-wood in the wrong hand.  "Let's have it, Joey.  You afraid you gonna show the girl your boner?"

Everybody but Joey laughed.  He glanced around with a pleading look, then seeing no one was on his side, not even Dwayne, unbuckled his pants and dropped them without a word.  He wore boxers with smiley faces and

Caroline shrieked with glee, clapping like a little girl who'd just seen Mickey Mouse at Disney World. He hurried his shot, bouncing the club up off the ground and clipping the top half of the ball, sending it to the rough on the left about eighty more yards ahead, well below Timmy Ray's and Mikey B.'s first shots.

Timmy Ray won the hole with a par, recovering a thousand of his dollars. He glanced over at Caroline as he got into his cart. Her nipples poked at her shirt, making little indentions in the cotton like they were struggling to get some fresh air. Then, seeing how well his new strategy was working, he thought of something else.

"Hey, Caroline," he said as he struggled out of his cart at the next tee box, stretching his thick arms out in front of him. "How much would it take to get a peek at those healthy girls of yours?" Nodding toward her chest, looking right at her perky nipples. "Ten? Twenty?"

"Excuse me?" she said, drawing her left eyebrow up, a crooked smile on her face.

"You know what I'm talking about." Timmy Ray still nodding his head.

"That wasn't in our deal." She crossed her arms over her midsection.

"I know. And I also remember saying that funny business was extra. So how much extra for a boob shot?" Secretly winking at her.

The guys gathered around Caroline, eager to see what it would take for the girl to show her boobs, the golf game all but forgotten. She paused, looking them each in the eyes, reading their faces, smelling their lust, seeing a way to make a hell of a lot more money than she had planned that day.

"A hundred."

"Really? A hundred?" Timmy Ray couldn't believe she was going for it.

She nodded, the devious smile still on her face.  Timmy Ray whipped out five crisp new twenties and she shook her head, saying, "No, a hundred from *each* of you."

Their eyes widened and they wanted to argue but they wanted the show more, each of them eventually reaching for their wallets and pulling out bills.

Four hundred dollars in twenties was shoved at her, the hands that held them sweaty and trembling.  The men were praying, hoping, *willing* her to take the money and lose the shirt.  She snatched the bills, one at a time, looking them in the eyes, one at a time, enjoying the power she held over them, lingering a little longer on Dwayne and Joey.

"I'm not sure this isn't some form of prostitution," she said as she stuffed the money into shorts that were so tight the guys could see the indentations of each individual bill.

"Don't worry," Timmy Ray said, leaning back against his cart, not sure he wouldn't lose his balance when she unleashed them things.  "Dwayne here's a cop.  He won't tell nobody, will you Dwayne?"  Dwayne shook his head, his mouth opened just enough everybody could see his tongue.

"Oh?  Really?  Well, at the least, I could get fired."  She looked around, up and down the course, seeing if anybody else was within sight.

The guys turned around, checking out the course, seeing nobody but a couple of squirrels, saying stuff like *it's cool* and *coast's clear* and *you're good*.  Caroline quickly grabbed the bottom of her t-shirt and pulled it over her head.  She stood there with her girls out in the open, not a tan line in sight, waiting for some kind of reaction before slipping the shirt back on.

Timmy Ray was the first to say something.  "Good God Almighty!  Them real?"

Caroline laughed, her boobs moving up and down with each breath.  "Yeah, they're real."

"Bull...*shit*," Mikey B. spouted off, "Ain't no *damn* way they's real and look that perfect." Shaking his head, still staring at them like he was unaware they were attached to somebody. "Ain't no fuckin' way they stay up like that, as big as they are, unless there's been some doctoring done."

"Oh believe me, they're a hundred percent natural." Caroline grabbed them and shook them around to prove a point, making Dwayne finally drool through his open mouth. Joey just stood there being real quiet and not moving, like he was turned to stone by Medusa herself.

"Prove it," Timmy Ray said.

She gave him a look like he'd just cut one, saying, "Now how can I prove I'm all natural? You see any scars?"

"They do wonders with surgery nowadays."

"Heh. Well, I don't know another way to prove it."

"Easy." He stepped forward, popping his fingers. "I've been to a million strip clubs and if I can't verify they're real, ain't nobody can." Wiggling his fingers, his eyes betraying his thoughts.

"Oh, *hell* no."

"Aw, come on. Don't be a prude."

"No. Not gonna happen. Not in a million years." Fingering her shirt.

"Aw, be a sport." Timmy Ray reached in his pocket and came out with another twenty. "How about another one of these?"

"*NO*." Then to put the matter to rest, she slipped her shirt back on, all the guys watching it stretch back out in the places it had to. "Anybody want a beer?" she asked like nothing had happened, bouncing over to her cart and opening the drink cooler. She sold four two-dollar beers to four really thirsty golfers.

"How about forty? Sixty?" Timmy Ray tried one more time before finally giving up, grabbing his driver and walking up to the tee box. With a smile on his face, he smacked his Titleist almost three hundred yards down the center of the fairway, over a kidney-shaped bunker that leaked in from the right side. It summed up the rest of his day beautifully.

* * *

CAROLINE FOLLOWED THEM out to the parking lot in her cart, pulling up right behind Timmy Ray and Mikey B. She stepped out and shuffled over to Timmy Ray with her hand out.

"Ah, yes. Money well earned," he said, counting off five twenties from his money clip and laying them in her hand.

She looked up into his face. "Where's the rest?"

Timmy Ray laughed, saying, "You'll get it. Don't worry. You think I carry that kinda cash around with me?"

"When?"

He shrugged. "When Dwayne and Joey pay up. Ain't talked to them about it yet." She was standing there, waiting for more than a lousy promise, shoving the hundred into her pocket, leering at him, waiting patiently.

"What?" Timmy Ray threw his hands up. "I ain't *got it.* What you want me to do? Look, stay here, I'll be right back." He left and walked over to where Dwayne and Joey were loading their clubs into Dwayne's Explorer, talked to them, then returned. "This Saturday night."

"*Un-huh,*" she said, the disbelief oozing from her voice. "Where?"

"Where you live?"

"No way," she said without hesitation. "Not my house. I'm not telling you where I live."

"What, you think I'd try to take advantage of you?"

She raised her eyebrows, not answering, letting him figure it out for himself.

He finally said, "*What?* I'm a nice guy, really."

117

"Yeah, right.  Nice guys don't carry around loads of cash in a money clip, offering girls money to feel up their boobs."

Timmy Ray shrugged.  "So I like boobs; sue me."

"You a drug dealer?"

Timmy Ray stopped and turned so he was facing her completely.  "That what you think we are?  Drug dealers?  *Jesus*, girl, you got some imagination."

It was her turn to shrug.  "What else would you be."

Timmy Ray looked at Mikey B, smiling real big like it was a funny secret, saying, "Hmmm … let's just say I'm in numbers."

"You're a bookie?"

Timmy Ray froze and raised his eyebrows.  "You're a smart one, ain't you?"

Caroline shrugged, still waiting for the answer to her first question, how she was going to get the rest of her money.  Timmy Ray reached into his Navigator and pulled out a business card.  He wrote his address on the back and handed it to her, saying, "Be there Saturday night, I'll have your money.  That okay with you?"

She looked at the card, reading where it said he was a Business Consultant, and laughed to herself.  She rolled her eyes, looked up, and said, "Yeah, alright, but no funny business."

Timmy Ray held his hands up like he was innocent of everything she was thinking, then she turned and went back to her cart.  Timmy Ray watched her perfect backside till she sat down in the driver's seat, then watched her drive off toward the clubhouse before he got in the truck.

"You gonna try and fuck her?" Mikey B. said when he climbed into the passenger's side.

Timmy Ray turned to him, smiling, and said, "I ain't gonna just *try*, pal. I'm gonna *get me* some of that college tang.  I always get what I want."

* * *

TIMMY RAY HAD IT all planned out.  He had a lasagna in the oven, keeping it warm 'cause he didn't know what time she was going to show up. He had candles on the dining room table, some of the good china set out that he got in the divorce, a tossed salad in the fridge, and a bottle of red wine.  It was a California Merlot the skinny fag at the wine store recommended to go with Italian food.

Timmy had done a lot of business that day; Duke didn't cover the five points that afternoon and like he planned, most people took them 'cause it was a home game at Cameron.  Them yelling college kids can only carry a team so far, he reasoned; you got to have the talent on the floor too.

He was in a good mood.  Everything was clicking; this would be the perfect end to a great week.  Caroline would show up and they would have dinner and—the doorbell rang.  Timmy Ray steeled himself, willing the butterflies in his stomach to scram, then went to the door.

"Hey," he said as he opened it.  He nodded with his head and said, "Come on in."

Caroline looked at him with her eyes narrowed, noticing his button-down shirt, a pair of Dockers and shiny dress shoes.  "Hello," she said as she stepped into the foyer and looked around cautiously, wearing a loose t-shirt and shorts and the same tennis shoes from the other day, no socks, the white leather contrasting her tan legs nicely.

"Please, come on in."  He motioned with his head to follow her deeper into the house, turning and walking off, giving her no choice but to follow. "I was just about to sit down to eat," he said as they entered the kitchen.  He went straight to the oven and opened the door, reached in with mitts on and pulled out the Pyrex dish of lasagna, closing the door with his elbow.

She cocked her head sideways, giving him a look he barely saw 'cause he was worried about dropping the lasagna before he could set it down.

Halfway to the dining room, he realized he should have gotten thicker oven mitts and wondered why the hell they made them this thin to begin with. He set the lasagna down quickly on a hot pad and shook his hands while biting back six curse words that immediately came to mind.

"I see," Caroline said, a smile creeping onto her face, "so you always cook a lasagna for one but set the table for two?"  She nodded at the table. On it were two plates and bowls with intricate gold designs, unlit candles and expensive-looking silverware. Timmy Ray had looked in a Martha Stewart Living magazine to see how the silverware was supposed to be laid out.  He even had triangular-folded linens in the center of the plates.

"Oh, well."  Timmy Ray smiled and shrugged.  "I thought I could thank you for a job well done.  You know, thank you properly, like a *gentleman*." He walked into the kitchen and pulled the salad stuff out of the fridge, grabbing all the dressings he had 'cause he didn't know what kind she'd like, and came back into the dining room with his arms full.

"Un-huh, like a *gentleman*."  She watched him place six different bottles of salad dressing on the table, shaking her head at him going to all this trouble to impress her.  "Well, if you don't mind, I'd like to just get my money and leave.  I appreciate all the fuss you went to—"

"It's my Granny's recipe," Timmy Ray interrupted, nodding his head toward the table.  "The lasagna.  She was a full-blooded Italian; came over on the boat when she was a kid.  It's an old world recipe.  I didn't use nothing from a can; it's all fresh.  She'd kick my ass if I ever used anything from a can in one of her recipes."  He paused and said, "You ever had *real* Italian food before?"

Caroline hesitated and glanced at the spread on the table.  Timmy Ray could see her resolve weakening, the enticing Italian aroma enveloping her, beckoning her to stay.  Garlic and tomatoes and melted cheeses wafting around the room now.

"Well, I *did* only have a bagel this morning," she said.

Timmy Ray disappeared back into the kitchen, grinning to himself, and brought out a basket, saying, "Even the garlic bread is homemade. Baked it this afternoon. My Granny's recipe too." He noticed this grabbed the girl's interest, her eyes widening a little and her eyebrows raising. He went over to her chair and pulled it out for her, looking up at her with his best puppy dog face.

Caroline scooted forward and sat down as he pushed the chair in. She said, "You didn't have to go to so much trouble, really."

"Are you kidding me? The way you helped me beat Dwayne and Joey? It was worth it. Not to mention the pocket change you made me." He shuffled over to his own chair, picking up the bottle of wine on the way.

"Yeah, but I made money too. How much is my share anyway?" Caroline said as she glanced around the room and played with her silverware.

Timmy Ray popped the cork with ease, not even paying attention to what he was doing. Then picked up her glass and poured it just below half full, and did the same to his.

"Uh, let's see. We won by five skins and I promised you half so you get twenty-five hundred. Plus that five hundred you raked in that you already got. Not bad for a day's work, huh?" He sat down in his chair and smiled at her, leaning forward and lighting the candles with a wooden match he struck on the table leg.

"Yeah, not bad but I guess it's a drop in the bucket for you." She was about to say something else but shut up when he nodded his head forward, closed his eyes, and began saying grace in hushed tones.

Caroline blinked twice, then closed her eyes and leaned her head forward.

"Yeah, pretty much a drop in the bucket but hey, money's money, right?" Timmy Ray said as he raised his head and took a sip of wine.

"You say grace?" It was out of her mouth before she thought better.

He laughed before finally saying, "Yeah, I say grace.  Something wrong with that?"  He reached forward and grabbed the salad, filled his bowl with the fork-spoon tongs, and handed it over to her when he was done.

"No, nothing wrong with it at all.  I guess … I just thought … I don't know, I mean, you're a bookie.  I just didn't picture a bookie saying grace, that's all."  Her face reddened as she took the salad and filled her bowl, reaching for the Raspberry Vinaigrette as he was squirting out Bleu Cheese dressing.

Timmy Ray shrugged.  "I give money to churches too.  That surprise you?"

Caroline raised her eyebrows.

"The way I see it is, churches provide services that can't be done by the government because the government hires people that don't give a damn whereas churches are full of people that care.  You tell me, if a church and the government were each gonna run an orphanage, who'd you rather give your money to?  Who's gonna take care of them kids best?"

"I never thought of it like that."

"But you know what I do that makes the real difference?  I make other people give to the church."

Caroline frowned.

"No, not like that.  As long as a church keeps my name confidential, I sometimes tell them that I'll match what anyone gives that day and then they announce it and you know what?  They get a record amount in that day. Cause something everybody understands is doubling their money.  And plus, it gets those people who were sitting on the fence, wondering whether or not to give, to go ahead and open their wallets."

Caroline smiled and shook her head. "But you're a bookie."

"So? What's that gotta do with it? Look at it this way: I take people's money who are using it to do something frivolous, like bet on a college basketball game, and I give it to people who really need it. And, of course,"—holding his hands out to the side, palms up—"I keep a nice little portion to live off of."

"Yeah, I can see that." Caroline looked around, still shaking her head. "I just don't … how much have you ever given at once?"

Timmy Ray shrugged and thought about it. "I dropped a couple hundred grand on a telethon about a year ago when I matched funds for ten minutes. Can you believe that? They were floundering away for half a day, barely pulling in a few lousy grand and in ten minutes, because of what I did, they raked in almost a half million."

Caroline narrowed her eyes. "See, that just doesn't seem like something a bookie would do."

"What can I say? Catholic upbringing sticks with you no matter what you end up doing for a living. Some of us are just better at making it work while others have all sorts of guilt issues. That's what religion's all about, ain't it? Guilt?" He shoveled a large portion of lasagna onto his plate.

"No, not really. I don't think so. Not guilt, per se. I think it's more about morals than guilt." She cut out a small section of lasagna and dipped it onto her plate.

"Morals? I don't see that; it's about guilt, making you do things they tell you that you *should* do, things they want you to do." He picked up the bread basket and took two thick slices out, dropping them on his plate. He handed her the basket while licking the garlic butter off his fingers.

"It's not about guilt," she repeated, taking the bread basket and pulling out a slice. "They don't use guilt to make you do things. The guilt's already in you; it's the good part of you that tells you when you're doing something wrong."

"See, now I think that's bullshit. Pure bullshit. It's all about guilt and population control. They want to tell you that you can't fuck till you're married, and then only with another Catholic, and even then you can't use a rubber. *Why?* Cause they want more Catholics in the world than anybody else. *Why?* Cause then they'll raise more Catholics. *Why?* So they can fuck other Catholics and have ten more kids cause they can't use rubbers and it just goes on and on."

Caroline paused. "So, which is it? Guilt or population control?"

"Huh?"

"You switched up." She held her salad fork in front of her, lettuce, red cabbage, and a cherry tomato pierced on it, vinaigrette dripping down into her lasagna. "You went from saying it's about guilt to saying it's about population control. So, which is it?"

Timmy Ray stared at her, wrinkling his forehead, watching her eat her salad and take a bite of her garlic bread. "It's both. Guilt *and* population control. They both work with each other. The guilt keeps you in line, keeps you doing what they want, and the population control is what spreads it everywhere. And really, if you want to get serious about it, it's about power and money. So forget guilt and population control, those are just the means to get to the ends. Power and money. That's the real pot of gold at the end of the rainbow." He rested for a second, replaying what he said in his mind, then smiled and dug into his lasagna.

Now Caroline was staring at him, her fork frozen inches from her mouth, eyes wider than usual, giving him a look he hadn't seen before. She said, "That's pretty deep for a bookie."

He wiped his mouth, saying, "Nah, that's what *everything* is about. Power and money. It always comes down to those two. The sooner somebody learns that in life, the better off they'll be. No stupid fuzzy illusions about the world."

They ate in silence now, Timmy Ray wishing he'd remembered to put on some soft jazz or rock, thinking that all this cooking might have worked and maybe he'd gotten her attention, but still chastising himself about forgetting the music. He might finally get to prove her bazookas were real, possibly touch other parts of her that were just as soft and tan.

As they ate, Timmy Ray watched Caroline sneak casual glances around his house: looking at the artwork, looking at the carpet, looking at the plush leather furniture in the living room.

Conversation during the latter part of dinner was sparse: Caroline saying here and there how good everything was, how she was going to have to get this lasagna recipe; Timmy Ray saying his Granny would kill him if he gave it away; Caroline remarking about the wine; Timmy Ray telling her it came recommended specifically for lasagna, saying it was a California Merlot, hoping that would impress her more.

Dessert was a chocolate mousse, another of Granny's recipes, Timmy Ray said, chilled perfectly in little dessert bowls with fresh raspberries on top, nestled in a dollop of real whipped cream. Timmy Ray said the Merlot was supposed to go with it, and it did.

After dinner, they moved to the living room, Caroline feeling a little tipsy, Timmy Ray feeling a little horny. They both sat on the couch, Timmy Ray on the opposite end from Caroline 'cause he didn't want to scare her away. They chatted, listening to music that he'd finally put on when he cleared the table, a rock band one of his "clients" recommended one time and brought to him as partial payment on a bet he lost. Some group called Second Saturday. Timmy Ray thought it was funny they were from Nashville and didn't do country; he hoped the girl would ask who they were so he could tell her and make a joke about them not being twangy.

"I had a nice dinner.  Thank you very much," Caroline said as she sipped her third glass of wine.  She couldn't believe she was actually admiring his taste in decorating as she looked around the room.

"You're very welcome.  It's not often I get someone so beautiful here to show off for."  Timmy Ray tried to make eye contact as he complimented her, wanting to see her reaction, wanting to see her smile at him, wanting to get the go-ahead signal.

Caroline chose not to say anything back and stood to look around the room.  What she noticed was an exercise in contradictions.  On one wall was what looked like an original Henri Matisse but she knew it had to be a reproduction.  When she touched the frame, Timmy Ray told her it was real, cost him thirty-five grand.  She flitted her eyes at him, then turned back to look at it again.

On the bookshelf next to the painting were books by all types of authors, ranging from David Sedaris to Nelson DeMille to Ernest Hemingway.  There were books on Vedanta, Christianity, Buddhism. Napoleon Hill. Martha Stewart. Bill Clinton.

"I got a signed first edition of *Bandits* by Elmore Leonard," Timmy Ray said in her ear. "It was only a hundred bucks, though."

"Oh?"

"Yeah, and look at this." He pulled a book out and handed it to her.

"*Thunderball*?"

"Yeah, it's signed by Ian Fleming and cost me twenty grand but it's not as good as *Bandits*."

Caroline returned it and started to pull out another.  *Pride and Prejudice.*

"Careful, that one ran me eighty-five grand. First edition." He waved his hand in front of it and she noticed his Rolex. Looked real enough.

Caroline shook her head and continued around the room. Beside the plasma TV was an African mask hanging on the wall and she almost asked about it, but then thought better. She didn't want to know. She sat back down on the couch and noticed for the first time a huge Bible on the end table. It was the size of her grandma's family Bible except this one was gilded in gold. She reached out and touched it.

"Beautiful, huh?"

"Yeah, it is." Caroline hoped he wouldn't tell her how much it was. He didn't. She sipped her wine faster now, wondering if she could still drive, then thinking it wouldn't matter when it came down to it, she'd drive anyway.

A minute passed before Timmy Ray asked, "So, you got anybody special in your life?"

"No, not really. I don't want to get tied down while I'm in school; pre-med is pretty tough and then after that, I got med school and I won't have *time* for a relationship." She sipped some more wine. "Besides, I have to work in my spare time to pay for it all. School loans only cover so much."

"That's a shame, a young woman like you shutting herself away from the world like that. You could make some man very happy."

"Oh, I don't shut myself away. I go out all the time. I date a lot, just not seriously." She looked him in the eye. "I don't want anybody holding me back, claiming me as their own." A pause. "I like my freedom."

"I believe you. You look like the free type. Won't take no for an answer when you want something bad enough. I'm like that, too. When I want something, I go for it. No matter what."

Caroline stared at him and said, "But sometimes you gotta take no as an answer; you can't have everything you want."

Timmy Ray sensed the moment coming, staring back at her, holding his wine glass on his knee. "Yeah, there's times you back off and there's times you don't. If you want something bad enough, though, you don't give up. You *never* stop. You don't take no for an answer."

"Nobody gets everything they want; sometimes there are things that are just off-limits, if you know what I mean." She took another sip while still keeping eye contact.

"I don't believe that. Willpower can be a strong force. It always comes down to who has the strongest willpower, and the most money. Power and money, just like I was talking about earlier."

Her eyes narrowed. "Not everybody can be bought, though, it isn't in their nature."

"Everybody's got a magic number," he said, barely sipping his wine, the glass hovering there for a few seconds.

"No, everybody has a limit, and they won't go past that limit, no matter what."

"I disagree," Timmy Ray said, his knee starting to bounce up and down. "It's been my experience that power and money can overcome anything, even someone's imaginary limits. A person has limits because they've never been offered anything to make that limit seem trivial."

She smiled, saying, "Now that's a load of bullshit if I've ever heard it."

Timmy Ray smiled back. "Not really."

Caroline sat her glass down on the coffee table in front of them. "I think I should be going now. Dinner was lovely. Thank your Granny for me." She got up and steadied herself, wobbling a little.

Timmy Ray got up, too, his smile subdued. "My Granny's dead. You're welcome though—"

"Oh, I'm sorry, I thought … "

"Don't worry about it; it was years ago."  Timmy Ray stood and waved his hand in front of him.  "But hey, there's no need to be rushing off.  Looks like you should wait a while before driving anyway."

"I'm fine, really."  She held her hand out to show how steady she was.  "Do you have my twenty-five hundred?"

Timmy Ray smiled and picked up an envelope off the coffee table, handed it over to her.  She took it and slipped it into her shorts as he said, "You not gonna count it?"

"I trust you … to a point."  She smiled real big, saying, "Besides, I know where you live."

"Sleep with me."  There, he said it, not as tactfully as he wanted and not at all like he planned but he was desperate; she was getting ready to bolt and it just came out.

Caroline raised her eyebrows, her smile dissipating as she dropped her mouth open, taking a moment before saying, "You don't beat around the bush, do you?"

"Lady, I've been beating around the bush for the last hour or so; now it's time to tell you exactly what I want."

"Oh?  I can see that, just blurted it right out, didn't you?"

Timmy Ray grinned, feeling the wine slow everything down a little, making everything fuzzy and cheery.  "Yep, and ever since the other day, I've wanted you more than anything in the world."

She shook her head and said, "Sorry, no can do.  Thanks for dinner though, it really was nice."  She moved toward the door.

"I'm not looking for a relationship or anything.  Just a one-time thing.  Just tonight.  A little hop in the sack, some meaningless sex.  No strings."  Timmy Ray talked too fast and slurred the last part.

"Sorry.  Look, don't take this the wrong way, but not even for a million bucks. Okay?"

Timmy Ray smiled, knowing everybody had their price, no matter what the girl said earlier; he knew it. He scratched the stubble on the side of his face, blinked twice, shrugged, then said, "How about *three* million bucks?"

This stopped her in her tracks. She was almost to the door and turned around to look him in his face. "Three million bucks? Yeah, right," she scoffed.

"No, really. Look in that bag there." Nodding toward a backpack in a chair just to her left, willing her to look in it.

She hesitated, peering at the bag, then walked over and unzipped it. Inside were bundles of hundreds, crisp and new like they'd just come from the bank. She looked up. "Where'd you get this?" she said.

"You really want to know?" His face tingled from the huge smile chiseled in it. He had her now.

"Yeah. No … wait, *yeah*, tell me."

"Some cop friend of Dwayne's made a bet with me, thought Duke was gonna cover their five points at home. I took bets with the guy before; he's known for betting more than he's actually got. It's landed him in some deep shit in the past. Almost lost a few fingers once." Timmy Ray raised his eyebrows.

He continued, "So I told Dwayne he had to bring it to me first, let me hold onto it, before I'd take the bet. He dropped it off last night and one thing I am is a man of my word."—bringing a hand to his heart—"Wouldn't have taken the bet if he'd gone with Carolina though; I knew they's gonna win, even at Cameron. And they did. Beat Duke by ten earlier today."

Caroline stood there with her forehead cinched up, her eyes slightly askew. "A *cop* bet this with you? And lost? Where does a cop get three million bucks?"

Timmy Ray shrugged his shoulders, drawing his mouth together, saying, "Where does anybody get three million bucks? I don't know, probably made a drug bust, cut a deal with the perp to let him go if he gave up the money or something. How would I know? I don't ask where somebody gets their money; hell, I don't *care* where they get their money, only that they got it. He had it. Now I got it. Now it can be yours. Just like that."

Caroline stared at the backpack for a few seconds before saying, "That's an awful lot of money."

"Not to me. It's just a drop in the bucket really." Timmy Ray crossed his arms. "But I know it's a lot for you. And it can be yours for just a little bit of your time."

* * *

CAROLINE STARED at the money, all those bundles of hundreds, tumbling over each other in the backpack, picturing her school paid for, picturing a big house instead of her crummy two-bedroom apartment with a roommate that never cleaned the bathroom, picturing a shiny new sports car instead of her beat-down Nissan Sentra with two hundred thousand miles on it that came off the assembly line when MC Hammer was still cool, seeing a chance to get her only living grandmother out of that decrepit nursing home that always smelled like cat piss when she went to visit.

"Just like that?" she said in a small voice, not looking up yet, still ogling all that green paper gathered in a blue Old Navy backpack with padded straps.

"That's what I said, *just like that*."

"Huh … just like that." She finally looked up at Timmy Ray, five feet from her, wine glass in his hand, bulge growing in his pants. She was thinking of the three million dollars, picturing it, savoring it, already spending it.

"Yep," he said. "Just … like … that."

She tilted her head sideways, looking him over, and said, "You think you can just buy me?"

Timmy Ray lifted his eyebrows and glanced at the bag.  "Three million bucks."

"And you think I'm the type to sell myself for some money?"

Timmy Ray repeated himself.  "Three million bucks."

Caroline looked at the money again.  She bit her bottom lip, looked up, and paused.  Then said, "What do I have to do?"

Timmy Ray sat his glass down and cracked his knuckles.  "Well, we can start by letting me verify if those jugs of yours are real or not."

135

"Money and success don't change people;
they merely amplify what is already there."

*Will Smith*

# #6

# Have Fun Tonight

"NINE-ONE-ONE, what is your emergency?" the voice on the other end of the phone said, a raspy voice that seemed to be somewhere between cigarettes number nineteen and twenty for the day, a husky female voice that lost its femininity about two grandkids ago, a voice that was firm and authoritative and none too happy to take an emergency call.

"Uh," Richard said into his phone, "you got any men operators?"

"Sir, what is your emergency?"

"Well, you see, it's kinda personal.  You ain't got no boss I can talk to?" Richard fidgeted on the couch, just wearing a pair of athletic shorts and his lucky Carolina hat with the N over top the C like it was one letter.  He was stretched out from armrest to armrest 'cause it hurt less when he laid like that.

"Sir, what is your name?"

"Richard."

"Your full name, sir."

"Richard Ferguson."

"Mr. Ferguson, what is the nature of your emergency?" the operator repeated herself, her voice steady and unemotional, like she could have been one of them computerized voices that tell you to press one if the problem is for the police, two for the fire department, three for an ambulance.

"You ain't got nobody else I can talk to?  Nobody that's, you know, a guy?  You see, the thing is—"

"Sir, Mr. Ferguson, the sooner you tell me the nature of your problem, the sooner I can send someone out to help you."  She paused.  "Are you currently located at 5602 Staley Farm Road?"

"Yeah," he answered, wondering how the hell this woman knew where he lived 'cause he sure as hell didn't remember telling her.

"Good, sir, now please tell me what your emergency is."

Richard thought about it a second, drawing up his courage, finally giving in 'cause he was hurting pretty bad.  "Alright, first you gotta promise not to laugh."

"Sir—" She sounded impatient now.

"You gotta promise.  That's the deal."

She paused, then said, "Okay, Mr. Ferguson.  I promise."

Richard took a deep breath, then another, then said, "It won't go down."

She waited a second before saying, "I don't understand, sir.  Can you be more specific?"

"You know, it won't go down … my wanger.  It's stuck."

"Stuck?"

"Stuck in the up position.  I got an *eee*-rection and it won't go down."

Richard thought he heard a snort in the earpiece, then she said, "Sir, are you trying to tell me that you have an erection that won't ... *return to normal*?"

"Yeah, that's what I'm saying."  Richard's face turned warm, almost as warm as his wanger was.

"And how long have you had this condition, sir?"  Her voice now not sounding as metallic as when she answered the call.

"I don't know ... a coupla hours?"

"A couple hours?" she said just a little too fast.  "Have you taken any medication lately?"

"You mean did I take one of 'em pills old men take?  Hell no, I ain't got no problem gettin' it up.  It just won't go back down.  What do I do?"

"Have you done anything different in the last twenty-four hours?  Eaten anything new?  Exercised a new way?"  She click-clacked on her computer while she talked to him, asking him a few more stupid questions he answered no to before she finally said, "Okay Mr. Ferguson, we have an EMT unit on the way.  They'll be there any minute."

"Thank you."

"You're welcome, sir, and ... *good luck*."  Her voice rose on that last part like she'd been holding her breath the whole time and just now let it out.

A commercial came on selling a turkey rotisserie that self-basted during the two hours it took for the thing to cook.  *Hehe ... basting your turkey.*  You could cook chickens, game hens, hams with the bone still in.  *Hehe ... bone still in.*  It came with a free bottle of liquid smoke artificial flavoring, a free carving knife, a free carving fork and four easy payments of thirty-nine-ninety-five and if you called right now, you also got a free cooking manual with over a hundred free recipes.  Richard already had the machine that let you grind up meat and herbs and spices and make your own sausage. *Hehe ... making the sausage.* He was dialing the 800 number on the screen when somebody knocked at the door.

"Mr. Ferguson? Are you in there?" a guy said on the other side.

*Thank God*, Richard thought, pushing the button to hang the phone up. He muted the TV, then said, "Yeah, come on in; the door's unlocked."

The door swung open and in walked a guy young enough to be Richard's little brother, and behind him was a girl even younger, both wearing matching uniforms: long blue pants with button-down long-sleeve white shirts. He hadn't expected a girl EMT; he hadn't even thought about it.

"Sorry we took so long, Mr. Ferguson," the girl said as she sat her toolbox down, not breaking her stride for a single second, even with him lying there on the couch tenting up his shorts like an overzealous Eagle Scout. "You didn't have any numbers on your mailbox down at the end of the road." She looked him straight in the eyes, purposefully not looking any lower, keeping her sweet little voice steady, keeping her sweet little face straight as an arrow like he was suffering from a bad cough instead of a permanent hard-on.

"Yeah, everybody around here knows where everybody else lives so I ain't never got around to puttin' the numbers back on." Richard thought about that Saturday morning three years ago when he was driving to the store to get some beer and saw his mailbox lying in the ditch, swiped clean off the post, a big ole dent in the side like somebody'd gotten drunk the night before and decided to play mailbox baseball. Never did find the stickers with his street numbers.

The EMT's shirts had patches with their names embroidered on. Jerry and Samantha. *Christ*, both of them younger'n him.

"Okay, Mr. Ferguson," Jerry said, "How long have you been like this?" Samantha pulled out one of those blood pressure bands and wrapped it tight around his left arm, telling him to relax and breathe easy.

"I told the lady on the phone, a coupla hours."

"Yeah, but we always like to double-check any information we get," Jerry said as Samantha put a stethoscope in her ears, placed the cold disk on the other end to the inside of his elbow, and began pumping the ball thingee hooked up to the blood pressure band.  "One time we went out to this guy's place, he told 9-1-1 his wife's water broke, only when we got there, she wasn't pregnant.  Nowhere near it."  Samantha was pumping that thing hard and the band was getting tight, way too damn tight if you asked Richard.

"Turns out she had lockjaw and had this contraption around her head. All it was, one of them wires broke, get it?  Her *wire* broke."  Jerry waited for Richard to smile at the wordplay and appreciate it as much as he did, his face stuck in a half-grin until Richard let him off the hook with a weak smile.

Samantha said, "So that's why we always verify everything we get called on, just in case."  She had been sneaking glances at his Coleman's Weathermaster while Jerry was talking, thinking Richard wouldn't know she was dying to see it, check it out herself.

She wrote his blood pressure down on a clipboard, ripped the armband off, put two fingers on his wrist, looked at her watch, and counted silently on her lips.  Her lips, red with lipstick, full, young.  They weren't helping his condition at all.  They were making it worse so Richard closed his eyes. But that didn't work, still kept seeing her pouty lips opening and closing.

"Have you taken any medication in the last twenty-four hours?" Jerry said, looking at his own clipboard.  *No.*  Have any allergies?  *No.* Exercised?  *No.*  The same set of questions he'd already answered on the damn phone, them wanting to get it right so he didn't turn out to have lockjaw or be pregnant.

"Well," Samantha said, still looking down at her clipboard, scanning it so she looked like she was doing something, Richard knowing she was just stalling to find the right words to say what was on everybody's mind. "I guess we should … " she started, leaving it open, hoping somebody would rescue the sentence, finish it for her. Richard waited them out, making them earn their money.

"Yeah," Jerry finally cut in, "I guess we should, uh, you know, take a look at your problem now."

Richard looked at them, his eyes innocent like he wasn't quite sure what they wanted.

Jerry reached out with his hands, then pulled them back like the act of uncovering the beast would provoke it to bite, saying, "Maybe you should, um, pull your shorts down yourself?" Ending it like a question, like Richard was going to have a choice in the matter.

So Richard obliged, thinking he'd put them through enough, ready to get his condition fixed 'cause it was hurting and he was supposed to be going out with his buddies tonight down to Handy's Bar, get drunk and maybe pick up a few women, screw in the back of his pick-up while looking at the stars. He grabbed the waistline of his shorts, lifted it up as high as he could so it wouldn't catch the top of his wanger, and pulled his shorts down gingerly.

*And behold, saith the people to the Lord, the Tower of Babel.*

Richard slid his shorts down past his knees before he settled back on the couch, his soldier standing at attention like it was roll call and the sergeant would stick him with latrine duty if he caught him slouching.

The girl EMT gasped when she saw it, her eyes widening like she was in sixth grade seeing one for the first time, like they'd snuck in the girl's bathroom during library and he pulled it out just for her. Jerry just frowned at it, chewing his gum quietly, gum Richard hadn't noticed Jerry had until now. Richard looked down at his thing, too.

"How long did you say it's been that way?" Jerry asked, still chewing his gum and frowning at the thing.

"Oh I don't know, goin' on four or five hours now," Richard said, looking at the Joe Camel clock over his TV, Joe's big sleepy eyes moving left and right with each tick-tock.

The girl stared at it with her mouth open, still not saying a word after that original gasp, Richard wondering if she was breathing any more.

"And what exactly were you doing when it first happened?" Jerry said.

This was what Richard dreaded the most, even more than a girl EMT coming out to the house, and he even considered lying about it 'cause what business was it of anybody's?  But then he remembered watching those reruns of ER and how the patients left out something embarrassing at first and their condition got worse and worse until they were almost dead.  Then they spilled the beans about what *really* happened and the doctors saved them in just a few minutes but they still had to lose a leg or a spleen 'cause they held out on their embarrassing secret.  He needed the quick-saving without losing any vital parts, 'cause he had plans tonight.  So he spilled.

"I's watching Katie Couric on the news."

"You what?" Jerry said.

"You know, Katie Couric?  Does the news?  On TV?"

Jerry didn't blink.  "I know who she is, you got *this*,"—nodding at his wanger—"watching Katie Couric read the news?"

"Well, not exactly.  See, there's this big hurricane coming into Florida and she's down there, reading the news outside while the wind blows her hair all around."  Richard looked down at his feet, not realizing till then it looked like he was staring at his wanger so he looked up.  "And well, that wind was gettin' pretty strong and her shirt was blowin' open and closed in the front, kinda like she was playin' peek-a-boo and then ... well,"—looking at Samantha who was still staring at his wanger—"You see, that wind was blowin' and it got her nipples all hard and you could see 'em pokin' through her shirt. And before I knew what was happenin',"—Richard looked back at his wanger, opening his hands like a car salesman showing a brand new feature—"it got like this."

Silence. Just the sound of breathing and the tick-tock of Joe Camel. Nothing else.

"Watching Katie Couric?" Jerry asked.

"Hey man,"—Richard getting testy now—"her nips got hard and she's not a bad-lookin' woman. A man could do a lot worse."

"I'm just sayin', man, the women on CNN and Fox are much better-lookin'. I mean, if you were watching one of them, I'd understand it a little better. Some of 'em used to be Miss Americas."

"Yeah, that redhead?" Richard said, pursing his lips together like he was gonna whistle, rolling his eyes around once.

"Yeah, now *there's* a hot one. I saw her nips hard once when she had an assignment in New York or somewhere cold like that."

"I was watchin' then! It was like a freak blizzard and she's standin' outside with no coat on and they just start pokin' out like they got something to add."

Jerry nodded, smiling, and said, "Yeah, man, I was watching at home that day and I got this huge-ass HDTV screen. Those nips were almost in my lap."

"Wow. Those HD things that much better?"

Jerry nodded, saying, "Way better, man. You can even see the little freckles on her nose where they didn't get the make-up on good."

The whole time, Samantha's watching Richard's wanger bouncing up and down, swinging back and forth, always coming back to rest, pointing straight up at the ceiling. Then she finally said what's been on her mind since Richard pulled his shorts down and gave the thing some air. "Is it always that big?"

Richard looked at it. Jerry looked at it. Samantha was still looking at it.

Richard thought for a second, saying, "I don't know; it hadn't crossed my mind."

Everybody looked at it in silence, the room as quiet as Sunday morning prayer, just Joe Camel tick-tocking the seconds away like it was Final Jeopardy.

"Gimme that tape measure," Richard said, pointing to the bar between the living room and the kitchen.

Jerry walked over to the counter while Samantha stayed put, still sitting there staring at the thing. Jerry searched around, finding car keys, a half-eaten package of Oreos, an empty bag of Wise sour cream 'n onion potato chips, two crushed Cheerwine cans, a bunch of mail, cut-out coupons, searching through all the mess till he finally found the tape measure under an old issue of NASCAR Weekly with Dick Trickle on the cover.

Jerry brought it back, thought about measuring the thing himself, then handed it over to Richard. Richard pulled the tape out about a foot, holding it up to his wanger, then put the end with the zero down in his pubes and squinted to read the number at the top. Then smiling, looked at Jerry and said, "Eight motherfuckin' inches." Smiling like he'd just won a year of free Bud Light from a scratch-off card. Smiling like a proud daddy who'd just seen his little boy hit a homerun out of the park for the first time, telling everybody around him that was *his* boy that done that. Smiling like he'd just asked the prettiest girl in the school to the prom and she said only if they got drunk and had sex afterwards, she didn't want to be a virgin no more.

"Jesus, man," Jerry said, "It always that big?"

Richard wanted real bad to say yeah but then remembered those ER episodes. "No. It's usually about six or so." Then added, "I guess."

"And Katie Couric did that?" Jerry asked.

Richard shrugged. *What else could he tell the guy?*

Jerry was still talking, "So, you try to … you know?" He held his right hand in a fist and jerked it up and down real quick, raising his eyebrows like they were sharing a private joke and Samantha wouldn't get it.

"Yeah, three times. Still won't go down."

Samantha finally broke out of her trance, saying, "Well, it looks like we gotta real life case of priapism here."

"*Pry-a-what?*"

"Priapism. That's when it gets hard and won't go down. Pretty sure that's what you got, alright. *Pry-a-piz-em.*" She said the word real slow, making each syllable real careful like she was in a medical spelling bee, Richard half expecting her to spell it out next. Like it was her word-of-the-day and she had to say it three or fours times in a sentence just to feel it on her lips, feel the way it rolled off them, like the word *effervescent.* Or *coercion.* Or *paraphernalia.*

"Well, what do I do to make it go back down?"

Samantha threw her hands up, saying, "I don't know, you try thinkin' of other things? Football or huntin' dogs or parachutin'?"

"Yeah, of course. After nothin' else worked, I thought of stuff to make it go down. My aunt Hazel." Thinking about her now, all three hundred pounds of her, never wearing any shoes, her feet two big calluses of thick dead skin, three warts on the left side of her face, her nose stubbed up like a hog's, always carrying a Butterfinger and a diet 7Up in her fat little hands.

"Paper factories." 'Cause he worked in one two years ago and it always stank there, almost as bad as Aunt Hazel after three days sweating in August with no bath. "Plumbing." 'Cause what's less sexy than a stopped-up toilet? Especially one Aunt Hazel's stopped up after hitting the Golden Corral buffet twice in one day.

"You name it, I thought about it. Look."

Richard pushed the mute button on his remote, pointing it at the TV so they all looked. "See that? This is what I was watchin' before you got here." The TV was showing a close-up of a chunky man's face. He was sweating hard and praying to the audience, looking up at the ceiling and waving his arms with his eyes closed. He ended with an *amen brother* and the shot opened up to a huge church choir, the words across the bottom saying it was Reverend Reid's Holy Baptist Grace Singers, and *O Lord O God Almighty* came blaring through the speakers. It wasn't a pretty sight, the Baptists not ones to wear much make-up and not care who they put in the front row, since God loved everybody the same.

"Yeah, okay," Jerry said, wincing. "We get the picture." He turned away from the TV and motioned for Richard to put it back on mute. "So I guess we need to take you in." Samantha nodded her head.

"What, you ain't got no pill I can take to make it go down?"

"Nope." Jerry shook his head.

"You mean to tell me they got pills to make it hard, but none to make it soft?"

"Not that I know of." Jerry shook his head again.

"Then how they gonna get it down?"

"They'll stick a needle in and take out the blood," Samantha said.

Richard didn't say anything, looking from Samantha to Jerry and back again to Samantha, only moving his eyes, his face as rigid as his johnson. Then he said, "I don't think so," while his eyebrows rose.

Jerry fiddled with the buttons on his shirt, saying, "That's what they gotta do or it could stay like that forever. Eventually kill you."

Richard thought about it a moment, realizing he didn't really have any choice in the matter. He'd tried everything he could think of. Finally he said, "Okay," then pulled his shorts up, being real gentle, pulling them up extra slow, *up and over*, making his Eagle Scout tent again; then reached for his lucky Motley Crüe t-shirt that was crumpled on the floor beside the couch.

They insisted he lay down on the gurney in the back of the EMT truck, 'cause it was procedure, and if they didn't make him they could get fired. Jerry drove while the girl rode in the back with Richard, hooking him up to machines, taking his vitals and his personal information, writing it down on her clipboard, asking him things like when was the last time he ate or drank anything, what did he eat or drink, when was his last bowel movement, nailing him down to exact times like he kept a Jenny Craig diary or something.

*Did she want to know how many ounces he shit? How big it was? Was it smooth or runny or hard? Did he grunt when it came out? Was it a two-flusher? On a scale of one to ten, how bad did it stink, one being Mary Poppins, ten being Rosanne Barr?*

The EMT truck swerved, swerved again, slammed on brakes, turned sideways, flipped, hit something hard, *real hard*. Scraping metal, burning tires, screaming Samantha, flying instruments, the world rotating funny, things hitting him, him hitting things, hard, *real hard*.

Then nothing, silence except for the EMT radio squawking, the motor idling. Richard was upside-down, still strapped to the gurney, feeling wet on his forehead, something sticking in his leg, laying on some beeping machine that was pushing his stomach in more than was comfortable.

He reached down and unhooked the straps holding the gurney to him, pushed it off him, got up on his hands and knees. Samantha was laying beside him with something sticking out her chest, not moving at all. Richard shook her, she still didn't move. He took her pulse, but wasn't sure what he was doing 'cause he'd never done it before only seeing it on ER, then put his ear next to her mouth, listened for breathing. Nothing. She sounded pretty dead; looked it too, her eyes half-open, not moving, glossy, staring at nothing in particular.

He crawled to the front cab. No better. Jerry was half in, half out of the windshield, his neck looking like it was one breath away from forgetting to hold his head on, a human-size Pez dispenser open all the way. No use checking for a heartbeat on him.

*Funny, these people supposed to help him, but not wearing their seatbelts.* Worried to death about strapping him in 'cause it's procedure but not giving a damn about themselves. Richard wondered if that was stupid or heroic? Maybe a little of both.

He climbed out the side door, anxious to see what they hit, or what hit them. He looked around, squinting in the bright sunlight, expecting to see dust or something in the air but everything was clear. Then realized something was different, real different, *life-changing* different.

He looked down. And there it was, or rather, there it *wasn't*. His wood was gone, his wanger back to normal size, like all he had to do was knock it around a little, slap it hard, treat it like a twenty-dollar crack whore, and it'd shake something loose, allow it to go from standing-at-attention to at-ease-soldier. No needles for him now!

Richard was so happy he momentarily forgot the two dead people who'd come to save him. Then, as he was jumping up and down, shouting at the world 'cause the little guy was flopping between his legs like it was supposed to, he saw it: the car they'd hit, head-on, now looking like it was half the size it was supposed to be, the girl driving it smashed against her steering wheel, looking like day-old hamburger with blonde hair.

The car, an old Nissan Sentra the color of puke, had its passenger-side door blown open and Richard went over to it. He looked in at the girl. She was still breathing, reaching toward Richard, clawing at the air between them. The radio played that eighties song, *Everybody Have Fun Tonight.* Richard sat down beside her and realized the girl wasn't clawing at him, but at a big golden Bible and a backpack on the floor. So Richard picked up the Bible, saying, "This what you want?" The girl was still not saying a word, clutching at the floor like her life depended on it, like she was having a heart attack and the medicine that would save her life was in the bag.

At least, that's what Richard thought, so he set the Bible aside and picked up the backpack. He unzipped it and looked inside, blinked, looked again, looked at the girl, looked in the bag again. He thought, *no fucking way*.

*Everybody have fun tonight ...*

He reached in the bag and pulled out a wad of hundreds bundled together, pulled another wad out, then grabbed hold of some papers and pulled them out.

*On the edge of oblivion ...*

They were legal documents, said *Bearer Bond* at the top. Richard riffed through them and added the numbers in his head. There was more than a million dollars on these papers and had to be at least another million in greenbacks. Maybe more.

*Everybody, everybody have fun tonight ...*

The girl was still clutching for the backpack, the documents, the money, reaching out like it was all she cared about, not the steering wheel shoved through her stomach, not the crumpled roof crushing her head between the dashboard and the headrest.

*Across the nation, around the world ...*

The girl sputtered out her last breath, blood bubbling down her chin, her right arm still outstretched for the bag. Richard smelled the alcohol on her breath now and it hit him all at once ... all this money was right there in his hands, with nobody around to say it wasn't his. It wasn't that far to walk home, not more than a few miles. And what was this girl going to do with the money anyway? Nothing; she was dead. It was as much Richard's now as it was anybody's. *Right? Finders keepers?*

He put the money back in the bag, grabbed the golden Bible, got out of the car, and slipped the bag around his shoulders, like he was going hiking. Hiking with a couple million bucks!

*Celebration so spread the word ...*

It started to hit Richard. All this money ... he could get him a new Camaro, or better yet, get him a mint condition 1978 Pontiac Trans Am with the original T-tops, like in that Burt Reynolds movie, and get that HDTV now, the biggest one Best Buy had, with surround sound and a separate bass subwoofer, watch Katie Couric in larger than life size.

*Everybody have fun tonight ...*

And then he realized he wasn't walking right, limping sort of funny. He looked down. And there it was. It was back, stronger than ever, harder than a steel rod, throbbing with each beat of his heart, the Coleman four-room special. *Shit.*

*Everybody Wang Chung Tonight ...*

153

"When it's a question of money,
everybody is of the same religion."

*Voltaire*

# #7

# Sweating Brother Bill

THE PREACHER talked about how we were all lambs of God, whatever that meant. From that, he slid seamlessly into a story from the second book of Samuel, a story about a rich man and a poor man with lambs, how the rich man had a bunch of them, and the poor man only had a female one. He called it a ewe. He fattened it up and gave it food and drink, not scraps like it was a dog, but regular food, treating it like it was his own daughter.

"There's a book of Samuel?" Agnes said, whispering in her hoarse worn-out voice, crinkling her face up as she leaned over in the pew close to Ruth, her breath still smelling like those two cigarettes she sneaked in the car on the way to church.

"There's two of 'em," Ruth said back.

"Two books? Of Samuel?"

"Yeah," Ruth said real quick, trying to listen to the good-looking preacher who was filling in for Reverend Darden 'cause he was on vacation for two weeks, on one of them cruises that took you up to Alaska and through all them icebergs and islands. Ruth didn't know what the big deal about Alaska was; it was just a bunch of snow and ice if you asked her. It wasn't like it was Hawaii or the Caribbean or Myrtle Beach, where there's lots of things to do and places to go. What's there to do in Alaska, count the penguins?

"Shhh," she finally said, trying her damnedest to pay attention to the substitute preacher, a young guy with a full head of wavy brown hair, a natural sparkle in his eyes, standing up there talking about lambs and ewes. He told people to call him Brother Bill.

From lambs of God to ewes as daughters and into James, talking about having patience, Brother Bill sweated and wiped his brow and preached about how trying your faith worketh your patience, that you should want nothing and not think that you'd receive anything from the Lord. He preached about being *bless*-ed, about holding true to your faith and letting nothing deter you from your righteousness, about being tempted with lust and sin.

"I could lust over him," Ruth said to Agnes, leaning over, raising her eyebrows, saying it a little loud 'cause the family of five in front of them heard her, the mother turning and darting her eyes back to see who said it. Ruth smiled at her, noting the woman's crow's feet, thinking to herself the mother could use a little collagen treatment that'd take ten years off her age.

The woman in front of them finally turned around minding her own damn business, and Agnes looked at Ruth, smirking 'cause she'd been looking at the preacher, Brother Bill, thinking the same thing, wondering what he was wearing under his preaching gown—a whole suit or just a shirt and dress pants or maybe just a shirt, a tie and boxer briefs—her imagination getting away from her now. Finally saying to Ruth, "Yeah, I know what you mean."

Both of them shared a conspiratorial smile, the same smile they'd shared at Club Zero the night before, staring at all the young boy-toys half their age dancing in tight jeans and unbuttoned shirts, sweat running down their faces and over their hairless chests. The two had picked a few boys out, trying to guess all kinds of things about them: how they kissed, whether they went both ways or not, whether they were virgins trying to act like they weren't, how big their schlongs were, how long they could keep it up. Stuff like that.

Those were the games they always played: dressing up in tight skirts, hose and silk blouses with wonder bras underneath that poked their freckled cleavage out there for all the boys to salivate over.

*Look out world, here we come, cougars on the prowl, searching for the next victim.* Agnes actually said that out loud once and it didn't sound as good as it did in her head—sounded kind of gay and Ruth told her as much—so she never said it again. She still said it in her head every time they went out 'cause it helped psyche her up.

Mostly, though, that attitude scared boys, them not having a clue what to do with a real woman that knew what she wanted and how she wanted it and her wanting it done to her more than five minutes before calling it quits. Boys that young couldn't keep much of a rhythm so the woman could get hers in; but lordy, they could get it up in three seconds flat and go several times in one night. Even if it did only last as long as a commercial break.

That was the difference. The difference between the young ones and the ones their age. Agnes and Ruth wanted to find some young studs to lock arms with, tote around like trophies, order into bed at a moment's notice, demand an instant erection and actually see it happen right then and there. One thing about those young ones though, they never got tired and they never got headaches, not like their first husbands.

Now this preacher, Brother Bill, was up there in his preacher's robe, getting himself all worked up talking about lambs and daughters and patience and lust and sin, and it was getting Ruth and Agnes all worked up watching him sweat, picturing him in tight jeans and an unbuttoned shirt, gyrating to some loud bass beat that was so deep it shook the clasp on your wonder bra. They watched him moving to his own rhythm, rocking back and forth, his wavy hair getting damper with each exalting word.

He was a little older than their usual fare, probably somewhere in his mid-thirties, but with that hair and charisma and energy, he could pass. There was just that one thing, him being a preacher and all. That kind of dampened the fantasy a little. It was pretty hard to dream about riding a man of the cloth, squeezing him between your legs every time you rose up. *Would you be able to make noises? Could you talk dirty? Was anal out of the question? Did preachers let you use a vibrator while they rammed into you? Did they like going down on you while you watched?*

These were important questions that affected the fantasy because for a fantasy to be good, *really good*, Agnes and Ruth believed there had to be the slightest chance it could really happen. If that was there, if you could picture it really happening, it was a good fantasy. Otherwise, it was just thinking.

Agnes said, "Should we go to the fellowship lunch today?" Meaning the potluck lunch held over at the fellowship hall every Sunday afternoon that Reverend Darden had started three years ago so all the shut-ins and elderly folks could have a real Sunday dinner the way God meant. A big ole lunch with fried chicken and roast beef and mashed potatoes and mac-n-cheese and deviled eggs and home-baked biscuits.

"You think he'll be at the fellowship lunch?" Ruth asked, nodding at Brother Bill.

"He's got to run it don't he?"

"Reverend Darden don't run it no more; Louise Ferrell does now."

"But Reverend Darden's always there."

Ruth thought about it a moment, listening to Brother Bill spout something about lust again while she was trying to focus, then said, "Yeah, I'd say he'll be there." Nodding her head while she turned back toward the front, catching a glimpse of that wrinkly mother in front of her twisting back around to face forward, having obviously been looking over her shoulder at Ruth without Ruth knowing it.

Ruth wanted to say something like, "Hey, if we're too loud for you, maybe you should take that stick outta your ass and put it in your ears," but thought that wouldn't be very patient of her, Brother Bill's words on lust and patience and sin actually getting through to her a little.

The rest of the sermon continued with Brother Bill preaching about lambs and daughters and patience and lust and sin, miraculously tying it all together by ten till noon, giving the choir time for one last song about Jesus and the announcements about Bingo night on Tuesday and the annual Chicken Pie supper next Saturday. Then the altar boys, accompanied on organ by Maggie Lawson, walked up to the front and snuffed the candles. At noon on the dot, the doors were opened and the bells chimed and Brother Bill greeted everybody as they filed out into the warm Sunday afternoon, stopping in groups to chat about what had gone on that week and how business was going and what was up with the price of gas and interest rates. Ruth and Agnes took their time when it was their turn with Brother Bill.

"Great sermon today, Brother Bill," Agnes said, standing closer to him than anybody else had, still holding on to his hand as they shook, not wanting to let go, seeing him wince as she breathed on him. She silently cursed herself for smoking those two cigarettes and then not bringing any mints or gum to cover it up.

"Thank you," Brother Bill said, nodding and shaking her hand. Then Agnes told him her name and he finished with, "Agnes, so good to meet you."

Ruth crowded her so she had to move on, and Ruth slid in as close as Agnes had, armed with that new Carefree Sugarless gum, the kind with the flavor crystals right in the gum that crunched when you chewed, her breath smelling sweet and pepperminty like she was skiing in the Alps. Saying, "It was a lovely sermon, Bill," dropping the Brother part so he'd notice her more, batting her false eyelashes like she was a horse shooing away some gnats, holding her gaze into his eyes, throwing him more signals than a sixteen year old slut in heat.

She gave him her name right before he said thank you, so he could add it on without waiting for her to say it. She held onto his hand, feeling how soft his skin was, staring into his eyes just enough to make him a little uncomfortable, and said, "Will we be seeing you at the fellowship dinner today, *Bill*?" Adding a lilt to his name, making damn sure he'd remember her out of the hundred new people he met today.

"Uh, yes, I believe I will," Brother Bill answered slowly at first, taken aback by her boldness, looking unsure of what to do next, but Agnes swooped in and pulled Ruth outside.

A fat man the size of a small Buick was next, his hands looking sweaty as they shook, Brother Bill saying, "Thank you for coming," like he'd said to every other person in line.

"What was that all about?" Agnes said to Ruth as they stepped into the sun.

"What was *what*?"

Agnes looked at Ruth like she was nuts. "Whaddya mean what was *what*? You practically molested him. If I'd had my eyes closed, I'd-a sworn I was watchin' a late-night movie on Cinemax."

Ruth raised her left eyebrow like she had no idea what Agnes was talking about, playing innocent like all she did was tell Brother Bill he did a good job and she'd never thought about ewes as daughters before. "I don't know what you're—"

"Cut the shit, Ruth." Agnes pushed Ruth to the side, lowering her voice and looking Ruth straight in the eyes, showing her that she wasn't going to buy into her act. "He's a visitin' preacher; what you think you're gonna do?"

Ruth's eyes hardened and she said, "All I did was flirt a little. Nothin' you didn't do."

Agnes' jaw dropped. "*Me*? You were almost feeling him up. I'd be surprised if he didn't go get a shower before comin' over to the fellowship hall."

Ruth rolled her eyes, puffed her cheeks out and blew a breath. "Right. Whatever, Mom."

"You still ain't answered me. What you think's gonna happen? He's a preacher."

Ruth shrugged, throwing Agnes a bemused smirk, then said, "He's still a man." Her giving one of her what-are-you-gonna-do looks, moving her head back and forth like a black woman telling her old man off, then she turned on one heel and started toward the fellowship hall.

The place was already half-crowded. The Ladie's Auxiliary worked in the kitchen, heating up all the food that people had brought in before Sunday school and preaching. Scrumptious odors filled the air. Chicken pie, honeyed ham, baked beans with bacon and onions, hot buttermilk biscuits fresh out of the oven.

Agnes and Ruth salivated, neither one had eaten more than a bowl of cereal for breakfast, expecting to go to a buffet in town for Sunday dinner after the sermon.  That is, until they got a load of Brother Bill and simultaneously decided to stay for the potluck dinner even though neither of them had brought one crumb of food.  Showing up empty-handed to a potluck dinner in the South was the eighth deadly sin.

"Oh, hi Agnes ... Ruth," Louise Ferrell said, a natural snarl molded onto her face, wearing too much make-up and perfume as usual, standing with her hands on her wide hips, her lazy eye floating off to the left like it did when she was looking for a fight.  President of the Ladie's Auxiliary and as close to an arch-enemy as anyone could be.  Catwoman.  Cruella de Vil. Fembot Number One.

"Hello Louise," Ruth said, projecting her best fake smile, the one she kept just for these situations, when she had to bite her tongue to keep from saying what was really on her mind.  Something like, "Which one of us you really lookin' at, Louise?  I can never tell."  Wanting to say it so bad her teeth hurt.

"You two stayin' for the potluck today?" Louise said with her eyebrows raised, like she was pleasantly surprised the two were there, like they were all old friends or something.  Then she said with her head cocked to the side, the lazy eye all the way to the left, "What did ya'll bring?"  Looking around to the tables with all the food on them, four long ones shoved together in a single line.

Agnes had already gotten a good look at the food and said, "Deviled eggs and ham biscuits."

Louise looked over at the food table, seeing the nine Tupperware containers of deviled eggs and six baskets of ham biscuits, then looked back, a huge smile plastered on Agnes' face.

"Oh," Louise said, then frowning, said, "Well, you two have a good dinner. I've got some things to do." She rushed off to play hostess.

Ruth poked Agnes. "That was quick of ya."

Agnes poked her back. "Nah, it was nothin'."

Then both of them saw Brother Bill and his perfect coif of hair walk in, and Louise scooting over to him with her arms out, like she was welcoming an old friend into her home for the first time. Ruth and Agnes watched the two of them talk and laugh, carrying on while Louise dragged him over to the plates and got him one, then started filling it up for him like he couldn't do it himself.

Ruth and Agnes sat as close to Brother Bill as they could—four chairs down—trying to get into his conversations, trying to laugh at his jokes about the preacher, rabbi and atheist, trying to get his attention when they could. But it was no use; he was surrounded by nothing but women, all trying to get his attention and catch his eye.

When it came time for dessert, Louise was one step ahead of them again, bringing Brother Bill a plate full of cake and banana pudding and butterscotch torte, throwing him her best flirtatious smile, showing off her caps like they were made of real pearls or something. She flashed her jewelry and flipped her hair and touched his arm and agreed with everything he said. And then afterwards, she left with him.

"Whore," Ruth said as they watched Louise and Brother Bill disappear out the side door of the fellowship hall, him looking behind them just before the door closed.

"Slut," Agnes said under her breath.

"Let's get outta here," Ruth said and they left without even cleaning up their plates, several of the Ladie's Auxiliary giving them stern looks as they walked out.

They were too pissed to go straight home, deciding instead to head to town to go shopping and get some double scoops of cookies-n-cream in a waffle cone. They were still talking about it when they came up on the man lying on the side of the road.

They stopped the car and got out. He wasn't moving, lying on his side with his back to them.

"Hey, you okay?" Agnes yelled like the guy was hard of hearing instead of dead.

Ruth got to him first and walked around him, afraid to touch him in case he was cold and clammy. He was laying there in a black Motley Crüe t-shirt, a pair of blue athletic shorts and some dirty running shoes without socks. She saw a big golden Bible clutched in an outstretched hand and when Ruth got all the way around him, she stopped and gasped, bringing her shaking hands up to her mouth.

When Agnes rounded him and saw it too, she shrieked and pointed and covered her mouth and pointed again. It was there for anyone to see if they'd come up on him. This man was lying on the side of the road, not moving, deader than a doorstop with his pecker pushing his shorts out like it was raring to go.

"Hey! You alright?" Ruth yelled for good measure, stooping over to get a closer look at his face. There wasn't any blood on him and he didn't really look dead; he looked like he was sleeping. She shook him and backed up.

He didn't move. Just stayed right there, slumped on his side. Shorts stuck straight out.

She shook him again and rolled him over on his back, his arm flopping onto the grass by his side, stirring up some ants that had made a train around him to a Burger King bag in the ditch. The other hand still held the Bible.

"That looks uncomfortable," Agnes said, noting the awkward position, then looking at his shorts bulging funny, thinking how much that must hurt.

"He's dead," Ruth said back. "He ain't feelin' nothin'." She looked at his shorts too, wondering how big that thing had to be to make the shorts tent out like that even after the guy was dead.

Both of them were crouched down now, looking at the dead guy, staring at his package, not saying a word 'cause neither one wanted to say what she was thinking, not on a Sunday afternoon after church. And not with him holding a Bible.

"What are you doin'?" Agnes said as Ruth reached out, her hands going right for the guy's waistband.

"What does it look like I'm doin'?"

"You cain't do that!"

"Sure I can; he ain't gonna mind," Ruth said as she snorted. She gripped her fingers snug under the elastic, looked at Agnes and said, "Don't tell me you don't wanna see it."

Agnes didn't say anything, just looked back at Ruth, thinking what Ruth was thinking now, *who's it gonna hurt to take a peek?*

Ruth turned back to the dead guy, lifted the waistband up and slowly pulled it back, blinking for a second before finally saying, "Damn."

Agnes just stared, her mouth drifting open, her face fixed somewhere between horror and amusement, looking at that thing stick straight up, the biggest one she'd ever laid eyes upon.

"You ever seen one like that?" Ruth said, nodding toward it, a smirk creeping across her face, watching her friend gape at it like it was Tommy Plott's and they were in the second grade when they played show-me-yours-and-I'll-show-you-mine. All three of them were in the coat closet in Mrs. Mim's class when the teacher opened the door, saw what was happening, and dropped the box of chalk she was returning, speechless except for a loud sucking noise that sounded like a donkey with a cold.

Ruth asked, "You wanna take a picture?"

"What?" Agnes said real quick, looking away from it, blinking and looking at Ruth.

"Come on, let's take a picture. Get your phone out."

"I … I …," Agnes stuttered, not reaching for her pocketbook, sweat beading on her forehead.

Then Ruth reached into the pocketbook and grabbed the camera-phone, pulled it out and flipped it open, and said, "Okay, fine. You hold his shorts."

Agnes still didn't move, shaking her head slowly, the look on her face headed more toward horror now than amusement, the lines in her forehead getting deeper by the second.

Ruth exhaled in a huff like she had to do everything herself, then held the camera-phone back a ways, pulled her hand out of the frame, steadied herself and clicked the button on the side, the thing flashing as it made a little camera noise like the cameras used to make when they took real film and auto-rewound after each shot. Then she took another just to be safe and make sure one of them came out right and not blurry.

"I guess we should call the cops now, huh?" Ruth said, turning to Agnes who was looking at the picture on the phone.

"Yeah," Agnes said, coming back to reality. "You think he's got any ID on him?"

"Shorts ain't got no pockets. Check his backpack." Ruth nodded toward the bag on the ground beside him, the padded straps still wrapped around his arm.

Agnes hesitated, then reached for it, pulling the zipper down and looking inside, freezing, looking again, mouth opening, jerking her head at

Ruth, jerking it back and looking one more time like it was going to be something different this time.

"What is it?" Ruth asked, craning her neck to look inside the bag, but the way Agnes was holding it, she couldn't see anything but shadows.

"It's … it's …," Agnes stuttered again.

Ruth took the bag from her, yanking it free of the dead guy's arm, yanking it just hard enough for some of the stacks of money inside to spill out on the grass.  Ruth stared at the money a few seconds, blinking, smiling, smiling bigger, then looked around making sure nobody was coming.

"Come on," Ruth said, doing some of the fastest thinking she'd ever done in her life.

"Come on what?" Agnes replied, watching Ruth grab the money, stuff it back in the bag and stand up, still looking around like somebody was watching them, testing them to see what they'd do.  *Be honest or take the money and run?*

"What are you doing?" Agnes asked as she stood now, half of her wanting to stay with the dead guy till somebody came, the other half wanting to follow Ruth and the money back to the car.

Ruth turned around when she opened the car door, yelling, "Come on!"

Agnes scurried to the car, then ran back to the dead guy and grabbed the Bible.  "What?" she said when she ducked into the car.  "It's a pretty Bible."

They sped out of there and took the money back to Ruth's.  It was almost three million dollars in hundreds and bearer bonds.  Neither of them had ever seen so much money in one place before.

They celebrated by taking a stack of the money to Ladie's Night at the Red Room, where a bunch of male strippers—twelve of them in all—came and strutted their stuff in leather thong pouches, their hard bodies drenched in baby oil.

Agnes went home with one of them, a six foot hunk with abs of steel and a pecker almost as big as the picture on her phone. She stayed overnight, doing it three times, making promises to buy him a new car if he could go one more time, throwing out hints that he could be her boy-toy if he played things right.

Ruth coerced two of the young Latino strippers, Raoul and Fernando, to take her back to their place for an all-night party of sinfulness and debauchery. Whipped cream, chocolate syrup and fresh habaneros from the potted plants on their back deck. They went at it until the sun came up, Ruth taking turns, boffing one while the other rested, having more fun than a commune full of hippies.

The women never spoke a word to anyone about what happened.

Agnes drug her new golden Bible to Sunday school the next week and received compliments from Reverend Darden, who had mysteriously returned from his cruise a whole week early. The word around church was that Brother Bill and Louise Ferrell had been interrupted by the Ladie's Auxiliary, doing something unholy to each other's bodily temples in the back room of the fellowship hall. Reverend Darden's sermon that week was an old standby he hauled out every once in a while about the evils of lust and gambling and money. Everybody knew who he was talking about.

Agnes and Ruth greeted him at the door with wide smiles, telling him that he'd been missed, asking him how his cruise was, did he see any whales or seals or penguins. He thanked them and said it was great—two whales and more seals than he could shake a stick at; no penguins though, him not having the heart to tell them penguins only lived near the South Pole—and flattered them on how stylish their dresses looked. The women said they'd had a little shopping spree at Belk's and showed off their jewelry: a pearl necklace for Agnes and a diamond tennis bracelet for Ruth.

"And did I see you pull up in a new car this morning, Agnes?" Reverend Darden asked.

Agnes blushed. "It's a Mercury Cougar."

He smiled. "Well, that color really matches your eyes."

"Mine's candy apple red," Ruth said, a grin spreading across her face.

When they entered the afternoon air, Ruth pulled Agnes to the side. "You know, that sermon of his gave me an idea."

Agnes half-closed her eyes and a smirk fluttered across her face. "What?" she said.

"Well, we've got lust and money under our belt," said Ruth. "How's about we work on the gambling?"

"Bingo night?"

"No."

Agnes shifted on the grass. "What've you got in mind?"

"You know that Indian casino up near the mountains?"

Agnes didn't answer. Her smirk melted into a big grin. She said, "Can we bring Raoul and Fernando?"

"Money won't make you happy . . .

but everybody wants to find out for themselves."

*Zig Ziglar*

# #8

# Toe Thumb

FRANKIE SPINKS dropped the plate of eggs and bacon and toast in front of her husband, not even blinking when the toast hopped onto the green Formica table.  A table that should have been thrown into the junk heap and burned but Eugene insisted it was a good table, only needed to be refinished.  Images of a beautiful lacquered wood creation crept into Frankie's head, but instead, Eugene found a piece of green Formica laminate at a salvage store and glued it to the top.  That was her refinished table.  It looked like shit, you asked her, but to Eugene, it was a masterful job.  He fancied himself a regular Bob Vila.

"Hey, careful with the plates," Eugene said as he snatched his toast from the table.  He looked at it a second and turned it over, then blew on it and took a bite.

Frankie watched Eugene eat, remembering how he wouldn't let her get any plates that were breakable 'cause they'd only have to replace them when they broke, so he made her get those heavy plastic kind from the Dollar General.  Had different pictures of hunting dogs on them; Frankie thought of fleas every time she ate off them.  Made her itch.

"We got a disconnection notice from the power company," Frankie said instead of saying what was really on her mind, wanting to tell Eugene exactly where he could shove those plates, and how far up he could shove them, and then what he could do once they were there.

"Whaddya tellin' me for?" Eugene said, his mouth full of toast and butter, crumbs falling on the table and in his lap.

"Cause I thought you'd wanna know."

"You the one that pays the bills, so pay it."

Franking stopped short and propped her hands on her hips, cocking her head to the side as she looked at Eugene's back, and said, "I ain't got no damn money to pay it with."

Eugene, not even looking up from his breakfast, came back with, "Maybe you oughta clean a few more rooms."

Frankie's face warmed and she wanted to explode but did a good job of holding it back.  Eugene was always talking about her maid job down at the HoJo's like it was commission or something.  Like she had some kind of control over how much money she made.  *How many times I got to tell him it's an hourly job?*

Eugene was still talking, "Or maybe get off your fat ass and get a second job instead of watchin' them damn soaps all afternoon."  He ate his scrambled eggs and crunchy bacon, making smacking noises with his mouth 'cause he wasn't ever taught to eat with his damn mouth shut, raised in a barn.  When Frankie's mama caught somebody chewing with their mouth open at the table, she'd slap them across the back of the head with her hand and tell them if they kept doing it, she'd smack their mouth closed for 'em.

"Maybe if you'd quit going out drinkin' all damn night," Frankie said as she stood behind him, thinking about doing what her mama used to do, "We'd have some money to pay some damn bills with."

Eugene said nothing; just sat there shoveling food in his mouth.

Frankie turned around and ate her breakfast standing at the stove, thinking if she sat beside Eugene, she'd lose it and try to smack his mouth closed. So instead, she stood and fantasized about killing him or at the very least, leaving him and running away with that tall UPS guy who always brought the stuff she ordered off those infomercials that ran early in the morning when she was getting ready for work.

Eugene got up, grabbed his dirty Carolina Panthers hat, the same one he didn't wear for a whole year after they'd screwed up that Superbowl game in the final minutes, saying at the time that he "wasn't gonna pull for their pansy asses no more." But the next season he was right there, parked in his recliner, downing beer after beer, wearing that ratty hat again, screaming at the TV every time they screwed up or made a good play. Frankie always said he had a memory as short as his johnny.

Eugene left his plate on the table instead of dropping it in the sink, put his hat on and opened the back door, saying, "And by the way, quit burning the damn bacon. You know I don't like it when—"

He ducked out just before the skillet and the rest of the eggs hit the door, cracking two panes of glass and leaving a nice dent right where his head was seconds before. He forgot his bologna and cheese sandwich. Frankie doubted he'd come back for it; still, she waited in the kitchen a few minutes more, hoping he would.

* * *

THE HOJO WAS just out of town on the interstate where all the tired drivers could stop and stay the night for thirty-nine-ninety-five, plus taxes and fees. Frankie clocked in and began stocking her cart with fresh sheets and toilet paper and towels and cleaning materials.

Marielena was the other housekeeper, a Mexican with five kids who was up here illegally and couldn't speak much English, but was the nicest person Frankie'd ever met. Always said thank you and please to everything. Frankie called her Marie for short.

"You day good?" Marie asked as she stuffed towels and sheets into her own cart, a perpetual smile plastered on her face, like nothing ever went wrong in her life. Frankie was almost jealous of her, except for her being Mexican. "It hurt this day?" Marie continued.

Frankie stopped and looked at her thumb that wasn't a thumb any more. Back a few years ago when she was married to her first husband, Harold, she caught him in bed with her best friend, Fayrene Harris. The skank had been after Harold ever since they moved into the trailer next to hers, making friends with Frankie just so she could get close to Harold.

One day Frankie came home early from the HoJo's, her stomach upset from some of them hot peppers Marie had brought in for their lunch break. As soon as she opened the front door, Frankie heard Fayrene neighing like a horse in heat. When Frankie got back to the bedroom, she saw Fayrene with her legs in the air, Harold between them giving it to her hard with nothing on but his Sunday black socks.

Frankie lost her cool, grabbed the first thing she saw, and went after them. That first thing was a cordless circular saw that Harold had in their room the night before when he'd cut some boards for their closet. She grabbed it off the dresser by the door, turned it on, and lunged for them both, screaming and cursing the whole way.

Harold and Fayrene reacted immediately, rolling off the bed and coming apart. Fayrene grabbed for the sheets to cover herself like Frankie cared about seeing her saggy boobs and beer gut. Harold grabbed his little willie, looking around frantically for his boxers and a way out, but he and Fayrene were both cornered with Frankie coming at them swinging the circular saw like it was a religious symbol and she was there to save them from the damnation of Hell.

Frankie wanted nothing more than to lop off Harold's willie so he could never cheat on anybody ever again. She went after him with that saw waving around and would've gotten him if she hadn't become tangled in Fayrene's massive bra lying at the foot of the bed.

Frankie fell forward, sticking out both hands to catch herself, one of those hands holding a rotating circular saw, the other holding nothing but air. She landed with her left hand outstretched, the saw slicing right through her left thumb at the inner joint. It happened so fast and she was so mad that she didn't realize it until she righted herself and felt the wetness of the blood all over her.

At first she thought she'd already got Harold's willie but then she saw him standing there, holding it like he had been earlier, eyes wide and staring, his naked body free of the blood she was seeing all over her hands. She looked over at Fayrene and saw the sheets didn't have blood, did the math in her head, then looked down at herself.

Frankie's scream was louder than when she interrupted Harold and Fayrene bumping uglies, and then she passed out. She found out later that Harold and Fayrene had gotten dressed and taken her to the emergency room and when the doctor asked where the thumb was, they looked at each other with their mouths stuck open. By the time Harold got back to the trailer, the thumb was gone, eaten by their beagle, Spike. Dog would eat his own shit if you let him.

The doctor gave Harold an option, since he was the husband and Frankie was still unconscious. They could do a radical procedure but it had to be done right then.

That was how Frankie ended up with a toe for a thumb, her first husband giving the doctor permission to go ahead and amputate the big toe off her left foot and move it to her left hand, 'cause Harold figured she needed a thumb more than a toe. When Frankie woke up from surgery, she was madder than hell and had divorce papers by the end of the day.

Now, the toe thumb ached every time a storm was coming and Marie thought that was amazing. She used Frankie as her personal weather channel, asking her every morning if it was hurting or not. Marie watched the news religiously and was constantly scared of hurricanes and tornadoes and thought if Frankie's toe thumb ever hurt really bad, that one of them big storms was coming and it was time to start praying to God as hard as she could.

"No, it's not hurtin' much today," Frankie finally said, still looking at her toe thumb. She wondered where Harold was now, whether he was still with Fayrene or had dumped her for a newer model.

"I go that way this day," Marie said, smiling and pointing toward the east wing, grunting as she pushed her cart forward. Frankie took the north wing.

The first three rooms had "Do Not Disturb" signs and Frankie cursed under her breath as she passed them 'cause now she'd have to come back later. She marked them on her clipboard as she came up to the next room. Its doorknob was bare.

Frankie inserted her key and turned the knob, yelling "Housekeeper" while she entered. The bedspread was on the floor and wet towels were strewn over the dresser and bed. She yanked the towels up and threw them in her cart just as a young man appeared in the doorway, wearing a pair of stiff jeans with a Red Man t-shirt and cowboy boots, his mullet parted down the middle.

"Fergot my phone," he said, looking around for it.

Frankie grabbed it off the nightstand and held it out to him as he walked over to get it, stepping on the bedspread like it wasn't there.

The man winced as he took the phone, saying, "What the hell's that?" He stared at her toe thumb like it was going to jump out and bite him, turn his regular thumb into a toe thumb too.

Frankie lowered her head and twisted away from him, trying to keep her mind on what needed to be done to the room. *Pick it up, change the bed, fresh towels, wipe down the bathroom, vacuum.*

The cowboy left the room and Frankie went back to cleaning. She'd just gotten in the bathroom when he returned, pulling a scrawny young woman in a ratty sundress behind him. "Show her," he said to Frankie. "Show Joleen your hand." Nodding toward Frankie and motioning with his hand to hold hers out.

Frankie stood there, looking at the young couple, a blank expression on her face 'cause stuff like this happened all the time. At the Tumble Wash-N-Dry. At the Shoney's breakfast buffet. At Stuckey's Bar on her darts league night where, when she lost, she could always blame the toe thumb and get a laugh.

Without thinking, she held it out, her toe thumb displayed for them like she was doing a commercial for hand cream, how it was the best cream in the world, made your hands look twenty years younger. She turned her hand over, and back again, giving the couple a real good look so their curiosity would be quenched and they'd leave sooner. Then she could get back to her cleaning.

"Oh honey, what happened?" the skinny woman said as she put her own hand to her mouth without realizing what she was doing.

Frankie gave them the short version, just telling them that her thumb got cut off and the doctors replaced it with her toe. That was it, nothing special.

"Does it still smell like a toe?" the man asked with a lopsided grin on his face. The woman elbowed him in the gut almost immediately, saying, "Stop it Sammy," but he still laughed like it was a funny joke.

Frankie'd heard it all. *Do you wear socks or gloves when it gets cold? Cain't nobody miss that if you ever gotta hitchhike somewheres.* She even got a can of athlete's foot spray at Christmas one year. "Hand" was written in magic marker over the "foot" part.

She turned away from them and went back to cleaning, raising her insult shield, trying her best to block out the sound of the man's voice from her memory. She could usually take anything that anyone said, laughing right along with them, saying stuff like she was the only person she knew could suck her toe while she went to sleep. She'd always join in with them 'cause it lessened the pain somewhat.

But today it was hurting, slicing through her heart like a barbed wire fence.

Frankie tamped the pain down and bottled it up, trying to look forward to two o'clock when her soaps came on. That was her time of the day, the one time she kept only for her and her alone. She'd relax at home, tuck her feet up under her, sit back with a cold glass of Coca Cola and a bowl of buttery popcorn, and enjoy a few hours of living somebody else's life.

* * *

"HOUSEKEEPING!" Frankie yelled as she turned the knob to #117 and pushed open the door. The room wasn't too bad—people's stuff still on the bed and dresser—but it didn't look as if anyone was here. Frankie left her cart blocking the door and began picking up the clothes on the bed and folding them neatly, then stacking them on the dresser.

The bathroom door cracked, then flew open, startling Frankie so much she almost dropped the blouse in her hand. A haggard-looking older woman stood in the doorway, her eyes red and still trying to focus and figure out what was going on.

"Who the hell are you?" the woman said with a scratchy gravelly voice like she'd smoked two packs of Winstons in the last hour. She steadied herself against the door frame and waited for an answer, her eyes still struggling to look straight at Frankie while her face contorted in small ways, like a cake bubbling in the oven before it finally hardened on top.

Then the woman's eyes widened and she fled back into the bathroom and slammed the door behind her. She started making the most awful yakking noises Frankie'd ever heard, Frankie hoping she hit the toilet 'cause Frankie would have to clean it up if the woman didn't. At least maybe aim for the sink or bathtub where Frankie could run the water till all the chunks gathered at the drain. Get it all up in one swipe with a rag.

As Frankie was staring at the bathroom door, listening to the woman retching out her guts, another woman in jeans and a pullover came through the hall door with a bucket of ice and two Ginger Ales. She looked at Frankie like Frankie was there to steal her stuff, like Frankie thought the puke-colored blouse she was holding was nice. Wasn't even made out of real silk.

"What the hell are you doing?" the woman said to her, setting the bucket of ice and drinks on the dresser while blocking the doorway.

Frankie was getting fed up with stupid people; the woman just had to walk around her cleaning cart to come in the room and now she's wondering what it is Frankie's doing there?

Frankie put the blouse down and said, "I came to clean the room."

"We ain't left yet."

"I knocked and nobody answered."

"You knocked?  Where's Agnes?" Agnes answered with a loud barf and moan from behind the bathroom door.  The woman looked at Frankie with big eyes, then said, "What'd you do to her?"

Frankie threw her hands up, showing they were empty, and said, "I didn't do nothin'; she's been in there throwin' up ever since I came in."

"You poisoned her!"  The woman pointed at her now, looking crazy with her hair everywhere and her eyes wide and bloodshot, like she'd been hopped up on something all night.

Frankie backed up because the woman came at her while still blocking the door.  If worse came to worst, though, Frankie was pretty sure she could take her, the woman looking like she was in her fifties, maybe her sixties.  Then the bathroom door flew open and Agnes stumbled forward, her face almost as white as the washcloth she was wiping her mouth with.

"You still here?" Agnes said to Frankie, talking like she'd told Frankie to scram right before she threw her guts up.

"I'm here to clean the room," Frankie said again, still hoping the Agnes woman had hit the toilet 'cause the smell coming out of that bathroom was enough to melt hair.

"She do anything to you Agnes?  She poison you?" the other woman said.

Agnes shook her head, then held onto the door frame like there was an earthquake.  "I just got sick, Ruth.  That's all.  I think it was that fifth margarita last night."

Ruth nodded, saying, "I told you to slow down but no, you thought you could hang with me.  You ain't never been able to drink like me."  Then pointing over to the dresser.  "I got some Ginger Ales."

Agnes moaned and held a hand against her mid-section, saying, "I think them wings and tequila is what messed me up."

Ruth brought her a Ginger Ale and said, "Here you go. This stuff does wonders." Then looking at Frankie. "Hey, you got any food around here?"

Frankie paused. First, the woman wanted to attack her, now she's asking where can she can eat. Frankie took a breath and said, "The Denny's down the street."

Ruth dug a hundred dollar bill out of her jeans pocket, shoved it at Frankie and said, "Won't you be a doll and go get us a coupla Grand Slam breakfasts? You can keep what's left." Winking her left eye at Frankie like they were best friends now.

Frankie frowned and thought, oh well, money's money. She reached out for the hundred, still not believing these two women, then figured it out. They'd been up all night gambling at the Indian casino and it looked like they'd won. Won big.

Ruth screeched and grabbed Frankie's hand, the hand that was reaching for the money, the same hand that had the toe thumb. Ruth held Frankie's hand out and yelled for Agnes to come get a good look at it, come look at the ugly thing.

"What'd you do to it?" Agnes said as scrutinized it, still not focusing her eyes like they're supposed to. "You mash it in a door?"

Before Frankie could answer, Ruth blurted out, "It's her damn toe! She's got a damned toe instead of a thumb!" Then she exploded into laughter while pointing at it.

Agnes burst into laughter too when she saw it was a toe and not a mashed thumb. "My God, it *is* a toe! It's really a toe! I cain't believe you got a toe for a thumb!"

Frankie jerked her hand back. Her face was as hot as that time she ate Marie's special peppers the woman said only the Mexicans ate.

Ruth laughed, saying, "What's the matter?  Cat got your thumb?" Slapping her leg and howling out loud like she was in a country western bar and somebody just fell off the mechanical bull.

Agnes laughed louder, saying, "At least she can say she's not all thumbs!"  Both of them howling now like those hyenas in *The Lion King*.

Ruth doubled over, holding her sides and making snorting noises, laughing so hard snot started to come out her nose, saying, "I give this movie one toe up!"

Frankie ran out of the room, tears streaming from her eyes, bumping into her cart and almost knocking it over.  She thrust it aside and limped down the hall, still hearing the women's laughter until she finally reached the storeroom and slammed the door behind her.

Times like this she wanted to chop her toe thumb off so nobody would laugh at her.  People never laughed at a missing finger but they did at one that was replaced by a toe.  It just wasn't natural.

She made up her mind right there that she was going to get that Agnes and Ruth.  She was going to get them good, even if it cost her job.  She was tired of taking shit and she wasn't going to take no more.  Not from Eugene. Not from Ruth.  Not from Agnes.  Not from nobody.

* * *

FRANKIE SET HERSELF up in the empty room across the hall from Agnes and Ruth.  She pulled a chair up to the bed so she could prop her feet up and rest her tired dogs like her daddy used to say.  He was a West Virginia miner and used to come in from a double-shift with his face as black as the coal he was digging up, then take a long hot shower, recline back in his lazy boy and prop his feet up so her mama could work the feeling back into them.  Frankie would sit at the kitchen table, eating her fried spam and mustard sandwich, watching the same thing happen night after night.  Her daddy called her his princess and he never would have laughed at her toe thumb, God rest his sweet soul.

It was well after two o'clock before the door across the hall opened and slammed shut a few seconds later.  Frankie was already standing, her hands moving nervously because she didn't know what to do with them till the women were gone.  In her pockets, on her hips, back in her pockets.  The waiting was agony.

And now Frankie was missing her shows; that made her even madder.  She had stewed all morning, going about her job quietly, thinking about everything she was going to do to their room when they left.  She ran all kinds of pranks through her mind, some she'd heard other maids had done and others she'd thought of herself.  For the last two hours, she holed herself up and did nothing but stare at her toe thumb to keep motivated.

Finally she opened the door and peeked out.  Nobody in sight.  She darted into the hall, opened their door, dashed into the room and stood there, looking around like a kid trying to decide which present she was going to open first.

She walked into the bathroom, straight to the counter, and picked up a toothpaste tube.  It was good old-fashioned Colgate, the normal white kind without all that extra stuff like tartar control and baking soda.  She unscrewed the top, pulled out a couple of mayo packets she'd gotten from the break room, and squeezed them into the tube.  Then screwed the top back on and mashed the tube around.

The other toothpaste was the blue gel stuff and that reserved its fate for the same thing Frankie had planned for their deodorants.  She fished a small vial out of her pocket, the same one that used to hold her wart medicine and when she ran out, she kept it in her purse because it might come in handy one day. Today was that day.

Earlier that morning, after the run-in with Agnes and Ruth, she asked Marie for one of her fresh habaneros, a yellow one that nobody but the Mexicans ate 'cause it could burn you inside-out and leave you gasping for breath like you only had one lung and a bad case of asthma. She split it open and soaked it in a cup with an inch of water. She left it there all morning, the water leeching all the heat from the pepper; then poured the liquid into the vial. Now she squeezed a few drops from the vial's dropper into the gel toothpaste and onto the roll-on deodorants. That'd teach those bitches.

Next Frankie pulled out a small bottle of liquid laxative and mixed it into their Dentu-Creme the same way she'd done the toothpaste and mayo. She poured in enough to keep them on the toilet for days till they figured out what was going on.

She went back into the room and stopped cold. There on the dresser was a big golden Bible, a nice one with the words "Holy Bible" embossed in cursive letters on the front cover. *These women?* Frankie couldn't believe they had a beautiful Bible like that the way they acted. Then she thought about what she was doing and whether or not Jesus would like it and that made her smile. She decided Jesus would laugh at the laxative in the Dentu-Creme.

She opened the closet door and smiled when she saw the nice dresses hanging there. She yanked them off the hanger, turned them inside out, and carefully cut some of the threads holding the seams. Now, when those bitches tried to squeeze their fat asses into them, the dresses would split open. Frankie chuckled, thinking how they would probably give up desserts for a month trying to lose weight, each one believing she'd gained ten pounds from the Grand Slam breakfasts.

Frankie dug a plastic baggie out of her pocket and looked at it with the awe a child does her first pulled tooth. Then she dumped the dead roaches from the baggie into the women's shoes. They were lined up in the bottom of the closet so neat it brought her extra pleasure to defile them.

Frankie lugged the suitcases out of the closet and hoisted them onto the bed. They were heavier than they looked. It made her wonder how many days they were planning on staying.

Ruth's name was etched into a metal tag on one of the suitcases and Frankie popped its latch open, figuring she'd start on hers first since she was the meanest. Frankie planned on maybe dousing the crotch of Ruth's underwear with some of that habanero water or maybe marking some of them with a brown magic marker, make it look like the woman had a case of the runs.

But Frankie never got that far because what she found in the suitcase stopped her short. There, piled in the suitcase right alongside Ruth's clothes were stacks of hundred dollar bills. Lots of them, nice and neat and crisp like they'd just come straight from the bank. There were more stacks than she could count and beneath them were some official looking bond documents and suddenly she forgot about giving Ruth a pair of real hot-pants.

She forgot about how much trouble her pranks could get her in. She forgot about her job and missing her soaps. She forgot about her no-good lazy son-of-a-bitch husband. And most of all, she forgot about all those bills at home, stacked up on the counter beside the toaster.

Then a thought occurred to Frankie and she turned and looked at the other suitcase. She popped it open and found more piles of cash. It was just sitting there, staring back at her, daring her to dream, teasing her, talking to her, whispering sweet nothings like a new lover courting her in the back of an old Buick. And in an instant, she knew what her future held.

As far as Frankie was concerned, she was buying an RV to travel the country. Maybe go see Old Faithful. Or Sea World. Or Dollywood.

She dumped the suitcase on the bed, then put all the money back in it, along with the money from Ruth's suitcase. Frankie didn't know how much it all was but she guessed it had to be a few million dollars. Whatever it was, it was enough to disappear with and never need to worry about anything ever again.

She snapped the suitcase shut and ran her fingers (and toe) over the edges slowly, savoring the last few moments of her old life. The life where everybody told her what to do. The life where she always came in last. The life where Frankie Spinks was the butt of everyone's joke. No, the *thumb* of everyone's joke.

That's something else she was going to do. Get another thumb. A *real* thumb. And it didn't matter if she had to go to Thailand or Brazil or somewhere crazy like that to get it. If it was the last thing she ever did, she was going to get a regular thumb. She ought to have enough money left over to see Dollywood and still retire to some cabin in the mountains.

She dragged the suitcase to the door and stopped. One last thing.

She opened the vial of habanero water and emptied it over Agnes's and Ruth's underwear. Emptied the whole damn thing, then squeezed everything out of the eyedropper too. Fuck 'em, she thought, fuck 'em all to hell.

"Certainly there are things in life that money can't buy, but it's very funny, did you ever try buying them without money?"

*Ogden Nash*

# #9

# For The Road

NICK AND WALLY drove around town, looking at Christmas lights, belching from the leftover turkey they had for lunch that day.

"That one's purty," Wally said, pointing at a two-story brick house with small twinkling lights along the eaves of the roof.  The lights ran up the chimney, all of them blinking in a train, like they had a pulse of their own.

"Yeah, it's alright," Nick said, thinking how he liked that six-foot Santa on the roof, perched beside the chimney like he was trying to climb it.  Two spotlights shined on him so people could see him from the road.  Nick thought how it would be funny if they had a couple of stuffed cops climbing ladders, guns on him like they were going to nab him before he broke in the place.

Then Nick realized whose house it was and decided he wanted that Santa for himself, take it home with him and set it beside the tree. He figured everybody and his brother was out looking at Christmas lights tonight though, so he'd have to wait until three or four in the morning to steal it. But the only way he was staying up that late was to get drunk and party with the Gordon sisters, maybe try and get some nookie from one of them. He wasn't staying up all hours of the night just to steal some stupid fake Santa off a roof.

They drove on, Nick feeling that itch inside of him he didn't quite know how to scratch.

* * *

"OOH, LOOK AT THAT ONE," Wally said, pointing at a house that had a full size sleigh with nine light-covered reindeer in front, the one leading the pack with a red blinking bulb for a nose.

"It's alright."

"That one's got all white lights." Pointing at another house.

"Yeah, it's nice."

"Look at that one, that tree's gotta be at least twenty feet high. Can you believe they got lights all the way to the top?"

"Yeah, that's cool."

Wally now turned and faced Nick. Nick was driving along not looking at anything except the road, his eyes not blinking, like he was one of them people on stage in a hypnotist act.

Wally's eyes tightened and he said, "This one's got Mother Mary breast-feeding a baby Jesus." Watching Nick as he said it.

"Yeah, looks good."

Wally punched Nick in the arm, saying, "You're not even paying attention, man."

"What the—*huh?*"

"I said you're not even watchin'."

"Yeah, I was thinkin'..." Nick turned back to the road.

Wally didn't say anything, waited for Nick to tell him what he was thinking about, waited a whole minute till Nick finally said something more.

"Let's go get some beers for the road," Nick said, still gazing straight ahead.

Wally started to say something, then turned and looked straight ahead. "Yeah, sure." He knew better than to say anything else 'cause whenever they started drinking this late, it didn't end up well. One time they woke up the next morning wearing women's clothes, their own clothes nowhere to be found. Another time, they woke up with hangovers he swore should have killed them and when they went to get some breakfast, the whole bed of the truck was full of fish, some of them still flopping around. Must have been at least a hundred of them, all different kinds.

Yeah, nothing good ever happened when they started drinking this late.

They stopped at the Quickie Food-n-Gas three blocks down. The store was almost deserted, just a few skateboard kids hanging around the energy drink section acting stupid and shoving each other into the coolers.

"Whatcha feelin' like tonight?" Wally said as they strode to the back, passing the potato chip bags and the candy bars. Wally made a mental note to get some of them new Wild Buffalo Ranch Doritos on their way out. They were ranch style with buffalo wing flavoring mixed in, commercials said they tasted just like you were eating hot wings dipped in ranch dressing and ever since he'd seen the first ad last week, Wally couldn't get them off his mind.

"I don't know," Nick said back without looking, keeping his eyes on the cooler with the beer and wine in it, walking straight there without wasting any steps.

"Let's get a twelve-pack of something."

"Sounds good to me."  Nick studied the selection, skimming over the ones that were on sale.  "Just as long as I get shit-faced."

Wally nodded and looked at the beer cooler.  "And let's get something we ain't never got before."

"Yeah, whatever," Nick said, staring at the big yellow signs.

"What about Heineken?" Wally said, pointing to the green bottles on the far right.  "We ain't never got no—*what*?"  Wally stopped 'cause Nick was frowning at him.

"You a fag now?" Nick said with his eyebrows raised.  "You gonna grow your hair long and wear an earring?  Get a butt buddy and stay home on Friday nights?"

"Whatcha talkin' about?"

"What am I talkin' about?  That's *fag* beer, man.  You wouldn't catch me dead drinking a *Hiney*-can."  Nick shook his head and gave Wally a look that made him feel like he was thirteen with a booger hanging out his nose.

"Well what kind of beer you want to get then?"  Wally closed the cooler door and looked at Nick.

Nick didn't answer at first and Wally felt like he did the time he caught Janie Thompson at her locker and asked her to the Senior Prom.  She stood there not saying anything, like Nick was doing now, her friends huddled behind her giggling till Wally finally walked away without an answer.

Nick looked at the beers again.  He scanned each row, left to right, right to left, top to bottom.  Took a breath and squinted his eyes.  Wally almost made a joke about what was behind door number two but he didn't want to get punched in the arm.

"Let's get some Natural Lite," Nick finally said, then opened the cooler and grabbed it so Wally would know that was the end of the discussion, they were getting Natural Lite.

* * *

FOR THE NEXT HOUR, Nick and Wally cruised around town, looking at Christmas lights and drinking beer. They stopped once to steal a blow-up angel and once to take a piss behind a manger set, Nick shorting out the floodlight trained on the three wise men and getting jolted so bad he pulled Mr. Wiggler back in his pants before he finished. He told Wally he spilled beer in his lap.

"We been through here already," Wally said.

Nick crushed the last beer can on his dashboard and tossed it out the window. "Yeah, I know that," he said as he slowed down and searched the neighborhood.

Wally said, "Well, whatcha lookin' for? I'll help." Then he belched so loud Nick got startled and tapped the brakes. Nick looked over at Wally like if he wasn't driving, he'd thump Wally on the nuts so hard it'd make his eyes water.

Wally shrugged. Then knowing that face Nick was giving him, put his hands in his lap.

Nick stopped the truck and pointed to the right, saying, "There. There it is."

Wally followed Nick's direction and said, "But I already seen that one. I showed *you*, remember?" Wally turned his head back toward Nick, half expecting Nick to punch him and say, *No duh dumbass.* But instead, Nick still pointed at the house.

Nick squinted his eyes and slurred, "We gonna get that."

Wally turned toward the house, then said, "What? That Santa?" Talking about the life-size one on the roof.

"Yeah, that fuckin' Santa, man." Nick nodded his head like there wasn't going to be any more conversation on the subject, same as he did with the beer. Then he turned off the truck and said, "Come on."

Wally shrugged to himself and got out, pulling up his pants 'cause he never had a belt that was the right size.  They were always too tight or too loose, never fit like the belts on the models in the JC Penny ads.  Of course, JC Penny didn't have models with a gut and cowboy boots.

Nick looked both ways before he scooted across the street, ducking his head a little like that made him less conspicuous.  Wally followed right behind him, copying the way Nick stooped his head over when he ran, but Wally stooped a little too much 'cause he never saw the curb coming at him.

He tripped and went face first into two plastic garbage cans, banging them with his head 'cause his hands were holding his jeans and he couldn't react fast enough to get them in front.  He hit the cans so hard that one bounced before it tipped over and spilled out, unused chicken parts and egg shells going everywhere.

Wally jumped up and shook himself like he had epilepsy.  He saw Nick clinch his fists and start forward like he was going to smack him across the head, tell him to calm down and get himself together.  But Wally, seeing the way Nick was looking at him, got the message and stopped, taking a moment to adjust his belt two notches tighter.

Nick turned and hunch-jogged to the side of the house where there were some big bushes to hide behind.  Wally followed, and this time, watched where he stepped so he didn't have any more surprises.

Nick was leaning on a ladder with a lopsided grin when Wally caught up.  "Lookie what I found," Nick said as he ran his hands up the ladder and back down again, like he was one of Barker's Beauties on The Price Is Right and he was showing off a brand new Dodge.

"Where'd this come from?" Wally said.

"It was already here, dumbass," Nick said as he reached out and thumped Wally on the forehead.  "Now get up there."

Wally rubbed his forehead, watching Nick point up the ladder.  His eyes grew big and he said, "Hell no!  I ain't going up there!  You gotta be *crazy* you think I'm climbing up that thing."

Nick folded his arms across his chest, saying, "Well *I* can't go.  You know I got that thing about heights."

When they were seven, Nick climbed the big magnolia tree in front of Julie Maynard's house to show off for her, but when he scrambled up there and looked down, he got a bad case of vertigo and fell like he'd been shot with a BB gun.  He broke both arms on the way down 'cause he was flailing about and screaming like a girl, managed to hit almost every branch.  Julie Maynard never did look at him the same after that.

"Well I still ain't going up there," Wally said.  "Ain't no way.  You know who's house this is?"

"Yep.  That's the point."

"Man, this is Troy Bowman's house."

"I know whose it is.  Didn't I just say that?"

"You wanna steal something from Troy *Boom-Boom* Bowman?"

Nick's eyes narrowed.  "Yeah."

"Man, you crazy.  We get caught, he's liable to beat the shit out of both of us just for shits and giggles."

"Well, let's not get caught."  Nick nodded at the ladder.  "Get up there."

"No way.  Hell no, man.  I remember what he did to those two freshmen who broke into his locker and pepper-sprayed his jock-strap."  Wally shifted from one foot to the other.  "It wasn't pretty, man.  Those guys probably still have nightmares when they get near a broom.  I heard one of them works at Walmart as a greeter 'cause he still don't walk right."

"Fuck Troy, man.  Mother-fuck Troy Bowman."  Nick got up in Wally's face.  "You remember what he did to me?"

Wally shook his head, his eyebrows lowering in thought.

"You don't remember Homecoming that year?"

Wally frowned as the incident at their senior Homecoming Dance replayed itself. A couple guys from the football team, led by Troy Bowman, held Nick down in the center of the gym and stripped him to his underwear. It wouldn't have been so bad except Jeannie Duggan had convinced Nick she'd give him a piece if he wore one of his sister's thongs to the dance. She told him thongs turned her on. It had been a set-up from the beginning and for the rest of the year, everybody called him Nicky. Troy even got the geeks on the Yearbook committee to print his name like that.

Wally knew enough not to say anything back and they just stood there staring at each other.

Nick took a deep breath and shook his head. "Come on, man," pleading now, "You gotta do it. For me. I need to do this, man, I *neeeed* it." Whining like he was five and begging for a candy bar at the grocery store checkout.

Wally frowned, saying, "That was eight years ago, Nick. Let it go. You don't need it."

Nick's eyes thinned. "Yeah I do. I need it so Charlene don't find out about that night last summer when you went skinny-dipping with—"

"Ah geez, man, why you gotta go there?" Nick had been holding that over Wally's head ever since he caught Wally and Linda Lou Jessup down at the rock quarry. Nick made him do things he didn't want to do 'cause Nick knew Charlene would kill him if she ever found out he'd played hide the turtle with her best friend.

"I'm just sayin', man. You wouldn't want Charlene to find out, would you?"

Wally bunched up his shoulders and took in a long breath, held it, then let it out when he realized he didn't have any choice.  He grabbed the ladder.  "You better hold this thing, man."

"I am," Nick said.  He laid a hand on one of the rungs and glanced around to see if anyone was watching them.

"That's all I'm sayin', man, just make sure and hold it good."  Wally now almost to the top, thinking to himself that something didn't feel right, that the left side was starting to sink a little.  Wally froze and looked down, seeing Nick looking everywhere but at him and the ladder, then feeling the ladder sink even lower on the left side.

"Hey, Nick?" Wally said, his voice sounding as wobbly as the ladder was getting.  "Nick?"

But Nick didn't get a chance to answer.  The ladder sank so far into the mulch that Wally's cowboy boots slipped and both Wally and the ladder went different ways.  The ladder landed on a bunch of azaleas and Wally ended up six feet straight down, on top of Nick.

Squirming and cussing, Nick pushed Wally off him and got to his feet.  "What the hell you doin'?" he said as he brushed himself off, then stopped when he saw he was spreading mud all over his jeans.

Wally sat up while he got his bearings, shaking his head like that would clear his cobwebs but it actually made him a little dizzy, so dizzy that he laid back down to stop the world from moving so fast.  Nick kept right on cussing and Wally didn't care one damn bit; he just wanted the world to slow down while he remembered who he was and what he was doing.  Thinking at the same time that at least he didn't get hit in the nuts.

"*Je-zus-Christ*, Wally, you tryin' to get us killed?" Nick ranted while Wally tried to get up by himself but the combination of six beers and a six-foot drop wasn't making it easy.

Nick helped him up, still bitching about how he wasn't going to get that Santa now 'cause Wally couldn't climb a damn ladder when Wally said, "Shit, man, let's steal something that ain't twenty feet in the air."

Nick looked at Wally and smiled.  "That's the smartest fuckin' thing I ever heard you say."  Then took off around the back of the house dragging Wally behind him.

Before Wally could say anything, Nick punched a hole in the glass part of the back door, reached in, and unlocked it.  They walked into the kitchen and Wally headed straight for the fridge.

"Whatcha doin'?" Nick said, stopping at the threshold of the living room and staring at the eight-foot Christmas tree with the lit-up Santa Claus on top.

"I'm gettin' another beer.  You want one?" Wally said as he saw a couple of twelve-packs on the bottom shelf.  "Whoa, man!  He's got Heineken!"

"What?  I don't want that damn *fag* beer, man."

"Don't worry, he's got some Bud Light here too," Wally said as he closed the door and went to the living room with a few beers in each hand.

Nick took the Bud Lights from Wally, popped one open, and like they did every time, clinked cans and downed the first beer together in one long gulp.  Nick crushed his can on his forehead and threw it to the floor.  Wally stared at him a second.

"What the hell, man?" Wally said, bending over and grabbing the can.

"What?" Nick said, shrugging his shoulders, popping open a fresh can.

"Why you gotta mess the guy's house up?"

Nick stopped in mid-chug like he didn't think he heard Wally right, then lowered his beer and said, "We're robbin' the place, man, and you want me to be neat about it?  We just tracked in a bunch of mud too, you gonna mop the floor before we leave?"

* * *

NICK STARED at Wally, waiting to see how he was going to answer.

Wally turned and walked to the kitchen mumbling something about putting garbage in its place. Nick shook his head and turned back around to the Christmas tree, wondering just how hard a bump Wally took outside.

When Wally came back to the living room carrying a fistful of beef jerky, Nick was holding the Santa that had been on top the tree, smiling like that time he'd gotten the air pump pellet gun from his uncle Donald. Donald was in the Navy and always got him presents that either shot things or cut them. BB gun, survival knife, compound bow.

Nick was still admiring his prize when he was snapped out of it by Wally, sitting cross-legged at the base of the Christmas tree, holding presents up to his ear and shaking them. Nick watched him pick up five or six more before finally saying, "What the hell you doin'?"

Wally looked up at him without missing a beat and said, "I'm listening to the presents."

Nick took one from him and ripped it open, saying, "Just tear the damn paper off, man, it ain't like it's yours or nothin'."

Wally's eyes grew real big like Nick just lit a Bible on fire. He reached for the present that Nick unwrapped, saying, "That's just mean, man, unwrapping somebody else's presents."

Nick wasn't believing what he was hearing and blinked a few times before saying, "Are you fuckin' *kiddin'* me? Did you just say that? You tellin' me it's okay to steal a man's beer and beef jerky but not his Presto Potato Peeler?"

Wally looked at the box in his hand, seeing it was one of them potato peelers you could only order off TV. He said, "Shit, man, I always wanted one of these!" Nick watched him turn the box over and read the writing on every side before stopping at the front again where there was a big picture of a funny-looking guy with a bushy mustache running a potato through the machine, showing just how easy it was to use that anyone could do it.

Nick shook his head, thinking he needed another beer before the urge to smack Wally in the head came back, then popped the top on one and downed half before sitting on the couch to watch Wally shake and open some more presents.  Nick looked around the room, trying to figure out how one person could own so much Christmas crap.  On the table across the room was a Santa with a sleigh and reindeer perched on top of a manger, baby Jesus laying inside with his hands up in the air like he wanted a ride.

Nick rolled his eyes and then noticed a crystal angel on the table next to him.  It gleamed and twinkled from the different-colored lights inside it.  He reached over and picked it up, surprised it was so heavy.  That thing wasn't cheap.

Then he looked around the room, seeing there was a lot of expensive decorations beside a lot of cheap shit, and began wondering why in the hell that was so.  He took a sip from his beer and turned back to see Wally open a turkey rotisserie.

* * *

AN HOUR LATER the front door opened and the living room light flicked on, waking Nick up where he was passed out on the couch, both his legs draped over one side with his muddy shoes still on.

"What the fuck?" a voice boomed from the entrance, startling Nick so bad that when he tried to sit up, all he accomplished was falling off the couch and onto Wally who was sprawled out below him in a nest of Christmas paper and beef jerky wrappers.  Wally woke up screaming 'cause the crystal angel Nick had in his hands landed square on Wally's nuts.  The guy at the door dropped low in a sumo wrestling stance, ready to tackle anybody that came at him.

204

Then the guy straightened up and scratched his head, saying, "Nicky? Wally? What the hell y'all doin' here?" A big grin broke out over his face. "I ain't seen y'all in forever!" Then he came over to where they were both trying to stand and wrapped them both in a huge bear hug, which wasn't too hard. He was six-four, two-forty and mostly muscle.

"Troy." Nick finally said when Troy let them go and Nick could breathe enough to talk. "What you been up to?"

"Hey," Troy said as he backed up and looked around, frowning at all the empty beer cans and unwrapped presents and muddy carpet. "Just what are y'all doin' here, anyway?"

"Aw, man, it's kinda funny," Nick said, sitting back down on the couch 'cause he was beginning to feel a little dizzy. "We got drunk and decided we's gonna steal the Santa off your roof but fat ass here"—pointing over at Wally—"fell off the ladder. Then we came inside to get some more beer and well,"—shrugging his shoulders and looking around—"we kinda got a little carried away." Nick raised his eyebrows like that explained it all.

Troy stood there, the frown stuck on his face, staring at Nick, not moving.

"It was just gonna be a joke," Nick said, feeling the need to say something more because his forehead broke into a sweat, looking at Troy in his brown UPS uniform, seeing how much bigger he'd gotten throwing fifty-pound packages around trucks twelve hours a day. "Like those wedgies you used to give the nerds in the chess club."

Troy smiled after a few seconds, saying, "Well, shit, fellas. Why didn't you say so? Tell you what." He looked around at the mess. "Y'all help me get this place back into shape and I'll let you live. The ball-and-chain's coming back tomorrow afternoon and I'll get killed if the house looks like this."

"You married now?"

"Naw. Frankie and me just got together not too long ago."

"Frankie?" Nick said, scrunching his face up like somebody'd let a stinky one out, looking around the room and seeing a bunch of girl stuff but hearing a man's name, thinking that explained the fag beer but still not believing Troy had changed sides, was playing for the other team now.

"Yeah, Frankie. My woman."

"Woman?" Still explained the fag beer.

"Yeah, her name's Frankie. But I wouldn't say nothing to her about her name … or her thumb."

"Her thumb?" Nick wondering just what in the hell Troy was talking about. "What about her thumb?"

"Huh?" Troy was looking around the room, taking in the mess Nick and Wally had made. "Never mind about the thumb. You smell piss?" Troy grimaced, then shook his head. "Look, we gotta get a move on and get this place back to the way it was. Frankie'll know if something's been messed up and I'll be the one to catch hell for it." Troy picked up a few beer cans and started toward the kitchen.

"So we gotta, like, wrap all these back up again?" Wally said, looking down at the presents on the floor.

"Yeah, we do," Troy said, matching up presents with wrapping paper and tags. "Or Frankie'll kill me … and then I gotta kill you." He stopped a second to look Wally dead in the eyes so Wally would know he wasn't kidding about that part, that Wally and Nick weren't off the hook yet.

Wally said, "Is it alright if we get a few more beers?"

Troy looked from Wally to Nick to the floor. "Why the hell not?" Troy said, "Go on and grab everybody a few while me and Nicky here get started." He slapped Nick on the back a little too hard, and handed him a box with a Santa sweater in it and some silver paper with candy canes and elves all over it.

"How you know this is for"—Nick looked at the tag still stuck to the paper—"Patty?" He positioned the box in the middle of the paper, trying to match the folds to the edges.

Troy frowned at Nick, then said, "Cause Patty's my sister, that's how."

Wally yelled from the kitchen, "Hey, what kinda beer you want, Troy?" Troy yelled back to bring him a Heineken and Nick looked at Troy like he wasn't the same guy that played middle linebacker in high school.

"What?" Troy said as Wally came back with three beers:  two Heinekens and a Bud Light.

"Nothin', man," Nick said, taking the Bud Light from Wally.  "It's just that, well, that stuff's for queers and women."  Smiling like he'd made a funny joke everybody would laugh at.

Troy raised his eyebrows and said, "Oh yeah?"  He gave Nick a look that made Wally smile, then said, "Well I guess you'll be a fag tonight 'cause you're drinking this instead of Bud."  He swapped his Heineken for Nick's beer and gave the Bud to Wally, telling him to go trade it for another Heineken.  He said, "Tonight, we'll all drink queer beer won't we?"  He looked at Nick, nodding and smiling, a vein on his forehead sticking out.

Nick managed to crack a smile and frown at the same time.  He popped the top on his can and took a small sip, tried not to gag, then pushed his eyebrows together and took a bigger sip, saying, "Hey, this stuff's not too bad."

"It's good shit, ain't it?  I used to always buy the cheap stuff till Frankie and me hooked up," Troy said as Wally came back in and handed him one. He popped it open and gulped like he'd just come out of the desert.

* * *

WALLY SMILED 'cause he'd never seen anyone boss Nick around like Troy was doing and it gave him more than a little satisfaction.  That, and Nick was drinking fag beer and liking it.

Wally walked back into the kitchen and yelled, "Hey, Troy!  You care if I grab somethin' to eat?"

Troy yelled, "Yeah, man, go ahead."  A pause.  "Anything but the cereal."

Wally glanced back in the cabinet he'd already opened, seeing the four boxes of Cap'n Crunch Peanut Butter Crunch, then thinking how good that stuff was and really wanting some, especially now that he couldn't have any.

Wally went back to the living room with a box of S'mores Pop Tarts, a jar of peanut butter and a Jethro spoon, saying, "Anybody want s'mores?"

Nick glanced up from the heart-shaped waffle maker he was wrapping. Wally held out the Pop Tarts, showing him that they were *real* Pop Tarts and not the cheap store brand they always bought, the kind that tasted like flour and blueberries, thinking how Troy must be making some good money at UPS to buy the real stuff.

"Yeah," Nick said, "throw me one."

Troy took one too, scarfed it down between gulps of Heineken, then grabbed another present.

They re-wrapped gifts for almost an hour, drinking Heinekens and talking about life since high school.  Troy said 'cause Frankie had money, he was quitting UPS after the holidays.  She was getting an expensive transplant operation in Thailand and then they were buying an RV and seeing the country.  Nick was still working down at the paper plant and hated his job; it always stank there.  Wally had a crush on some chubby girl who worked in the supermarket deli.

The Pop Tarts and peanut butter only masked Wally's hunger.  He went back to the kitchen for some more food and stopped to look at the Peanut Butter Crunch again.  He thought Troy probably wouldn't miss some from one in the back. He opened the cabinet door right as Troy brushed beside him, and he almost peed his pants.

"Whatcha lookin' for?" Troy said as he pulled a couple Heinekens out of the fridge.

"Huh?" Wally said, jerking his head around. "I don't know, just lookin'." His eyes landed on something that looked so nasty it had to be good: honey and mustard Vienna sausages. Wally thought that if Troy had them, they couldn't be so bad.

Then Wally saw something he didn't believe, a bag of Wild Buffalo Ranch Doritos, sitting right there in the cupboard like Troy had bought them just for him, like Troy had known that Wally would forget to buy his own in the store that night.

* * *

"HEY," WALLY SAID four fag beers later, "I got a problem over here"—everybody looking—"I got two boxes that's the same size and two wrapping papers that match. Which goes where?"

Troy said, "Well what's in the boxes and what's the names on the tags?"

"Um, I got a pair of nose trimmers in one and a big-ass pink scarf with reindeer on it in the other."—looking at the tags—"And the names are Aunt Susie and Robert."

Troy looked at Wally for ten whole seconds without blinking or making a face, waiting for him to figure it out by himself. Then he saw that Wally wasn't even trying, was staring right back at him with a blank face like Troy's old dog Charlie Daniels used to. Dog was dumb as a tick; would stare at him for hours without making a sound or even tilting his head. Made Troy wonder if dogs could be retards or not.

Troy waited for what felt like a full minute more to see what Wally would do before finally shaking his head and saying, "The scarf goes to Aunt Susie." Then he returned to the Speak-n-Spell he was holding, thinking how it wouldn't be a bad present for Wally if he was going to give Wally a present.  But he wasn't.  Wally was lucky Troy wasn't going to beat the shit out of him and Nick for all the mess they made.  Then he wondered if he needed to tell Wally the trimmers went to Robert.

* * *

NICK SHOOK WALLY AWAKE a little after eight in the morning while he kept a hand over Wally's mouth.  He said Wally's name real soft like Nick's mama did the night they split to Salisbury for a week to give his daddy "time to cool off."

Wally opened his eyes and blinked a few times, his expression changing from fear to recognition, then nodded to Nick.

"You ready to go?" Nick whispered while looking around the room.

Wally nodded again and sat up.  Nick held a bulging bag and Wally asked if Troy gave it to him.

"No, now shut up and come on," Nick said, looking over at Troy passed out in the lazy boy, the chair reclined all the way back with Troy's big feet sticking up like a dog's ears at attention.  And for the first time, Nick noticed the Rolex sparkling on Troy's wrist.  The sun poured in through a crack in the curtains and lit it up like it was on display just for him.

"What's in there?" Wally whispered, nodding at the bag as he stood.

"*Shhh ...*"

Wally kept quiet till they got to the kitchen, then he said in a low voice, "It's the light-up Santa from the top of the tree, ain't it?"

"Would you shut the fuck up and get out the damn door?" Nick said, pushing Wally forward, still looking around like Troy was going to catch them sneaking out.  Thinking about how hard it would be to slide that Rolex off his arm, then shaking his head.

But Wally twisted away from Nick and scurried back into the living room, Nick watching him with his mouth wide open, wanting to scream at Wally but knowing he couldn't without getting his face rearranged by Troy.

Wally came back a few seconds later and followed Nick out the back door, stopping when they got outside to say, "Hold on, take this." He thrust a present into Nick's hands.

"What's this?" Nick said, shaking the gift as Wally disappeared back into the kitchen. Nick watched him with his mouth wide open again, thinking about just dropping the present and taking off without Wally, letting him take his own chances with Troy.

But Wally came back out before Nick could make up his mind about leaving. He carried a stuffed brown grocery bag in both arms and sported a silly grin that took up half his face.

"What the hell you get now?" Nick said. He strained his neck to look in the bag but it was too close to Wally's body.

"I got some food."

"Food? You went back to get food?" Nick thought real hard about thumping Wally on the forehead but couldn't 'cause his hands were full.

Wally reached in the bag and dug out two Heinekens, saying, "I got some for the road," still smiling as he handed one to Nick.

Nick shook his head and smirked. "Man, you're crazy. You know that?" He took the beer after stuffing Wally's present under his arm, but the present slipped and fell to the ground.

"Hey, man! Careful!"

Nick frowned, replaying the sound the box made when it hit the ground, then said, "It's that gadget, ain't it? You went back and got that damn potato peeler."

Wally nodded and said, "You bet I did, and look what else." He held the brown bag out so Nick could look in.

"Cereal?"  Nick couldn't believe what he was seeing, wondering if his eyesight was going bad or maybe he was still drunk.

"This ain't just any cereal, this is *Peanut Butter Crunch*, man.  This is the best cereal in the whole goddam world.  I love this stuff."  He sat the bag on top of the potato peeler and picked them both up in his arms, then followed Nick to the car.

Nick was still shaking his head when he slid into the driver's seat, thinking Cap'n Crunch was good but not good enough to risk your life over.

They started the truck and they took off, heading home to the other side of town, but after a couple blocks, Wally said, "Man, I gotta pee."

Nick looked over at him, thinking it wasn't that far, and said, "Hold it."  He looked back at the road.

Wally began fidgeting, saying, "I don't think I can, man.  I *really* gotta go."

"Why didn't you piss in the bushes at Troy's?"  Nick wanted to get back home and crash in his own bed, curl up and pass out for half a day.

"I didn't have to go at the house.  It didn't hit me till we got in the truck."  Wally was really getting fidgety now, moving around like he was getting ready to have a baby, Nick thinking he better not break water in his truck.  Wally said, "My pants are too tight."

Nick took a deep breath and closed his eyes for a split second, then said, "Well loosen your damn belt."  Thinking how hard could it be?

Wally unhooked his belt and let out a breath.  He leaned back in his seat a little, then looked over at Nick and said, "It didn't work, I still gotta go.  Real bad."

"You can wait," Nick said, not taking his eyes off the road.

"No, man, I can't.  I really can't."  Wally held his johnson and squeezed it like he was two years old and stuck in the supermarket, waiting for his mama to take him to the bathroom in the back stockroom where all the employees went.

"Jesus, man!  You gotta be kiddin' me!" Nick said as he slammed on the brakes and swerved into the parking lot of a Circle K.  He came to a stop fast enough to throw Wally's grocery bag into the floor.

Wally jumped out of the truck and ran inside, snatched the bathroom key from the kid at the counter, then ran back outside and around to the bathroom, holding up his pants 'cause he'd never buttoned them back.

Nick shifted the truck into park, leaving it running so he could warm it up, and popped the top off his beer.  He took a swig, then reached over for one of the cereal boxes on the floor.

Nick picked it up with a frown on his face, thinking unless this cereal had an actual jar of peanut butter as a prize, it was way too heavy.  He opened the top and stared at its contents, then put the box aside and picked up another one from the floor.

It was just as heavy.

He looked inside, then picked up the other two boxes.  All four were the same, each filled with stacks of hundreds and official-looking papers, the money bundled together perfect like you saw it on TV shows.

Nick was still staring inside the cereal boxes when Wally returned with the color back in his face.  "Ahh," Wally said as he opened the door and climbed in.  "That feels better."  Then seeing Nick with his cereal boxes, all four open beside him, he said, "You like that stuff too, huh?"

"You look inside these yet?" Nick said, holding a box up, not waiting for an answer as he turned it over.

Wally opened his mouth to yell but froze when he saw the bundles of money falling all over the seat instead of Peanut Butter Crunch.

"Where'd that come from?" Wally said after a few seconds.

"All these cereal boxes full of it.  All of 'em full of money."  Nick looked at Wally, then said, "You couldn't tell they was heavy?"

Wally shrugged, saying, "I was in a hurry."  Still staring at the money, thinking, then looking up and saying, "So, there wasn't any cereal at all?"

Nick didn't answer.  He wondered what they were going to do now, 'cause Troy might not miss the lighted Santa or the potato peeler or a few extra beers, but he was sure as hell going to miss all this dough.

"How much you think's here?"  Wally said, picking up a bundle. "What, maybe a couple hundred thousand?"  He held it close to his ear and fanned it out like guys did in movies and then they'd say it was missing a hundred and who's got it?

Nick crinkled his forehead and picked up a stack, did some counting in his head, added it together and multiplied by this many and that, added in the numbers on the papers that said "Bearer Bonds", and finally said, "At least a couple million I guess."

"A couple million?"  Wally's mouth dropped open.

Nick thought some more, knowing Troy's woman didn't get this kind of money legally, and even if she did, she wouldn't be keeping it in some cereal boxes.  She'd put it in a bank.

Still on that line of thinking, Nick figured out Troy wouldn't be calling the police; he'd come for them himself, kick their asses for real, maybe even worse.  They couldn't go home now.  That would be the first place Troy looked.

Wally sniffed the money and held it front of him, smiling.  "So how long you think a couple million—"

"Shut up, I'm trying to think," Nick said.

"Think about what?"

Nick looked straight into Wally's eyes, giving him a deadpan face that let him know to shut the hell up or else. Wally threw his hands up and went back to fanning the money out next to his ear.

Nick slid the truck in gear and backed up, saying, "We gotta go. We gotta leave town."

Wally frowned and paused. He said, "Wait, can we stop and get something to eat?"

Nick looked both ways and pulled out onto the road. "You mean to tell me you're still hungry?"

Wally shrugged, saying, "I was gonna snack on Peanut Butter Crunch but now there ain't none, and since we ain't going home, can we stop somewhere?"

"I ain't stoppin' for nothin'," Nick said.

"That Circle K we just stopped at had food. We could—"

"We ain't going back." Nick stared ahead as the truck accelerated.

"How about that Kroger's?" Wally pointed out the window. "They're open."

Nick realized Wally wasn't going to shut the hell up till he got some food in him. Nick whipped the truck into the Kroger's parking lot without slowing down—doing it fast so Wally would know Nick was pissed off—and slammed on the brakes right in front of the doors instead of parking in a spot.

"Hurry the fuck up," he said.

Wally put the stack of hundreds down, opened the door, stepped out and turned around, saying, "You got any money? I ain't got my wallet with me." Slapping his pants legs as he said it.

Nick stared at him, waiting for him to figure it out by himself, raising one eyebrow to give him a hint, then looking down at the seat 'cause Wally still wasn't putting two and two together.

Wally followed Nick's eyes, smiled, and said, "Oh yeah."  He laughed as he pulled a hundred out of the bundle he'd been holding, then said, "I'm gonna get some Peanut Butter Crunch, you want anything?"

Nick thought for a second, then said, "Yeah, we got a long drive ahead of us.  Get a couple twelve-packs of them Heinekens."  Nick pronounced it right this time instead of saying *Hiney*-cans, waited for Wally to smile, then added, "For the road."

"There's a phrase we live by in America: "In God We Trust".
It's right there where Jesus would want it: on our money."

*Stephen Colbert*

# #10

# Channel Ten

TRAVIS PUSHED the cart around behind his grandma, hoping none of the guys from school had any reason to be at a grocery store on a Saturday morning. He'd catch hell for a whole week if any of them saw him shopping for control-top pantyhose and Dentu-Creme.

The guys were probably down at the courts, shooting some hoops or something, jawing about who they went out with last night, bragging about who got some and whose date had Fort Knox legs. Anybody saying they got laid was probably lying through his teeth anyway, trying to make himself look cool, when all he got to do was cop a feel under the girl's shirt with her bra still on.

Grandma Baxter took five whole minutes to choose a box of oatmeal, settling on a variety box with maple'n brown sugar, apples'n cinnamon, and peaches'n cream.   She took another two minutes to shuffle through her coupons to see if she had any for oatmeal, found she had one for Quaker instead of the Kroger's store brand, then spent another minute doing the math in her head, and finally picked the store brand anyway 'cause it was still a nickel cheaper, even with the coupon.

They reached the cereal aisle and Grandma Baxter paused.  "Travis," she said in her rickety old voice that skipped a syllable every once in a while, "You can get any cereal you want and if your mama gives you any guff about it, you tell her I said you could have it."  She ended the sentence on a head nod and face scrunch that made her thick glasses slide down her nose a half inch.

Travis grabbed a giant box of Peanut Butter Crunch immediately, 'cause even though he wasn't seven any more, he still looked forward to his box of Cap'n Crunch every time he went with Grandma to the grocery store. It was a ritual now.  She always told him he could get a box of cereal and he always picked Peanut Butter Crunch.  And she always said if his mama gave him any guff, he was to say Grandma said he could have it.  His mama never gave him any guff.

On the canned goods aisle, Grandma Baxter stopped to scoff at the price of canned green beans, huffing at them 'cause she grew her own every summer and canned them herself.  She kept them in her dirt-floor cellar where a single light bulb hung from the unfinished ceiling.  The room was damp and spooky and Travis always felt like he was going to step on a snake or a possum every time she sent him down there to get a mason jar of veggies for one of her stews.

"Hey, Grandma?" Travis said as he inched the cart behind her.

Grandma Baxter looked up from her price scrutinizing, squinted at him through her glasses, and said, "Yes?"

"How come you don't get one of them laser eye surgeries?  You wouldn't have to wear them Coke bottles any more."  He smiled like he cracked a joke she never heard before.

Grandma Baxter cackled out loud and said, "Lordy, Travis, why'd I wanna go and do that?  I ain't got many more years from meetin' my maker.  Why in the world would I wanna go and start fixin' things up now?"

Travis felt uneasy every time his grandma talked about dying like it was just another trip to the grocery store instead of a trip to the hereafter.  He stood there looking down, counting the number of diamond patterns in the floor.

Grandma Baxter continued, "Now if'n you had an old car on its last leg and it had a busted radiator that did just fine unless you took it on long trips, would you spend all that money to get it fixed up?  Of course you wouldn't; you'd just not go on no long trips.  That's the good Lord's way of tellin' you he's about to reclaim what's rightfully his."

Travis closed his eyes, wishing he hadn't gotten her on one of her religious rants, then remembered that it didn't matter what he talked about with Grandma Baxter, she always turned it around to preaching about Jesus and Heaven and God's will.  It was never failing.

For ten more minutes, Grandma Baxter droned on about living a good Christian life so you could go to heaven, preaching to Travis even though he never did anything wrong except miss church a few Sundays a year because he felt like he was "saved" enough that week and wanted to sleep in.  He thought Jesus would understand.

Grandma Baxter was still going on when they arrived at the register.  She counted out her coupons while Travis loaded everything on the conveyer belt.  As the checkout girl ran it all through, Grandma Baxter hawked the computer screen, making sure all the right prices came up and the coupons rang true.  They were worth double today.

Travis rolled his eyes at the girl when he knew his grandma wasn't looking and scored a smirk from her. He wondered if there was any way he could work that smirk into getting a date 'cause she wasn't all that bad looking. He was pretty sure she was a grade behind him in school but didn't know her name until now. Her tag said *Claire.* He'd have to remember that, say hey to her in the cafeteria, ask her how things were going and make a joke about his grandma.

Travis pushed the cart through the automatic doors ahead of Grandma Baxter 'cause he always made a game out of racing her to the car and loading the groceries before she got there. He won a little over half the time depending on whether or not you counted dropping the cart off at the cart corral as part of the game.

But this time there was a truck blocking the down-ramp with a guy inside banging the steering wheel and cursing so loud Travis could hear him through the windows. Travis had to swerve at the end of the ramp to miss the truck, then go all the way around its back end, whereas Grandma Baxter could squeeze between the truck and the post and head straight for the car. *Damn.*

Travis gripped the handle and sprinted from the curb, pushing the cart as fast as he could, then stopped it inches from the old Chevy Caprice. He yanked the driver's door open, hit the automatic locks, and threw the grocery bags in the back as fast as possible without letting them tip over.

Travis finished moments before his grandma got there and felt a sense of accomplishment that even though God had seen fit to throw a big rusted truck in his way, he'd still been able to pull out a victory.

* * *

GRANDMA BAXTER, aware of the game Travis liked to play, had slowed her walk down to almost a crawl to give Travis more time, remembering that last time he hadn't won. Jesus would want the boy to win about half the time and she wouldn't do anything Jesus didn't want.

But then, right as Travis was handing her the keys, two guys carrying grocery bags approached them. She recognized the chubby one on the right as the guy who was in line behind them at the checkout, and the other as the guy in the pickup truck blocking the downramp.

"Howdy," the driver said, wearing a big cheesy grin that made him look like he was trying to sell them something off a late-night infomercial.

Grandma Baxter squinted behind her thick glasses, sensing something wasn't quite right but not knowing what it was, then she wrinkled her nose as she smelled the beer on the man's breath.

The man continued, "It looks like we done run out of gas and we's wondering if you'd let us borrow your car." The chubby one behind him chuckled.

Grandma Baxter felt tingling in the back of her mind as she remembered a convenience store hold-up she once witnessed. A guy had come in waving a gun around, threatening everybody in the place but heaven had sent an angel to watch over them. A sweet young man in line took charge and talked the robber out of doing anything. She'd never seen anything like it. She looked around the empty parking lot; there was no angel there for her this time.

Grandma Baxter held out her purse and said, "Take it, just don't hurt us."

The man laughed hard, saying, "We don't want your money, you old biddy. We just want to borrow your car for a little while on account of our truck being out of gas." Then he took the keys from her hand while his buddy threw his bags of groceries in the back and went around to the passenger's side.

* * *

TRAVIS FELT SICK 'cause he couldn't stop them but both guys were way bigger than him and he wasn't too sure what he could do anyway. He watched them drive away with his grandma's car and all her groceries, anger slowly building up in him as he replayed the scene in his mind over and over, wondering if he could've done something like they always did on TV. Maybe karate kick one in the knee and the other in the nuts, yell to his grandma to jump in, and then hop behind the wheel and squeal out of the parking lot.

"Well, I guess we should go in and call the police," Grandma Baxter said, bringing Travis back to reality.

The cops pulled up a few minutes later 'cause they were just down the street at the Krispy Kreme getting jazzed up before their morning shift. Travis thought it was funny they each got out of the cop car with a doughnut and a coffee cup when that was something people always made fun of cops for, and yet they still go and do it. Like they couldn't help it. Like how yankees drive fast and queers wear tight jeans.

"Alright, what seems to be the problem here?" the short cop said, taking a second to sip on his coffee.

Grandma Baxter squinted her eyes and craned her neck toward the cop. "Somebody done stole my car, Officer … *Fasting*? What kinda name is that?"

The tall cop snickered and jabbed his jelly doughnut at the short one's gut, saying something about never fasting a day in his life.

The short one frowned. "Um, it's Officer *Faustino*, ma'am. And it's Italian; means *lucky*. And this is"—the other cop was laughing so hard he dribbled jelly on the front of his uniform—"Officer Crawford." He gave his partner a steely look. "He's not the swiftest cow in the meadow but he'll do in a pinch."

Travis and Grandma Baxter gave their statements and witness descriptions to the cops even though they already said the same stuff to the cops on the phone. Travis told them so but the two cops still made them repeat everything just in case they missed something before. Like Travis would suddenly remember the big one had a tattoo of a swastika on his arm or the other one had a glass eye. Something that would break the case and one of the cops would smile and say he knew exactly who it was, been causing trouble all his life, had a rap sheet a mile long.

Then they asked all kinds of stupid questions that Travis couldn't see made any difference 'cause Travis had already told them that was their truck right in front of the store, telling them to just go look at the registration in the glove compartment and run the license plate through their computer. The tall cop came back with just making everything official, crossing their T's and dotting their I's.

At some point, the short cop looked at the other and said, "Betcha twenty bucks we never see the car again."

The other one, Officer Crawford, stuck his hand out and shook it, saying, "You're on. The way your luck is running, I can't lose." Then he looked at Grandma Baxter and said, "Ms. Baxter, what color blue would you say your car was? *Carolina* blue or *Duke* blue?"

Officer Faustino's face turned red at this and he went to check out the truck while the tall cop laughed and returned to his squad car, not even sticking around for Grandma Baxter's answer.

Ten minutes later, still waiting for the cops to finish up their paperwork, Travis thought about how he and Grandma Baxter were going to get back home and whether or not they were going to buy more groceries first, 'cause even though Grandma's car was stolen, she still needed milk and eggs and stuff.

The cop radio started squawking and the cop in the car got excited. He jumped out and spilled his coffee, saying to everybody they found the car. Held out his hand to the short one until he coughed up a twenty. It was down on Market Street right across from the Lube World, smoke coming out from under the hood.

The cops gave them a ride and on the way there, Officer Faustino said, "Hey Ms. Baxter, betcha twenty the keys are still in it."

Grandma Baxter opened her mouth to say something, thought about it, then said, "Young man, betting is immoral. It's blasphemous and I'll say a prayer for you tonight."

Officer Crawford laughed and Officer Faustino turned back toward the front without saying a word.

When they got there, smoke was still pouring out the front grill of the car. The two front doors were wide open like on the TV show "COPS" when the guys bail out and start running, thinking they can get away from the helicopters and the cameras and thirty cops behind them.

Office Faustino popped the hood and smoke engulfed him. He waved it away, looked inside, then came over to them.

"Looks like a busted radiator," he said, wrinkling his brow and pursing his lips together. Travis thought he looked a little like a short Barney Fife with a beer gut.

Grandma Baxter smiled, saying, "Well I'll be." She looked at Travis and pushed her glasses up on her nose, saying, "You see what I mean, Travis? You see what I mean? You heard him, didn't you? It's a busted radiator. You remember what I's saying to you earlier about busted radiators?" Grandma Baxter shook her crooked finger at him. "It's God's will, I tell you. It's God's will."

Travis stood there with his hands in his pockets, not sure if this was one of them one-sided conversations or if he should be answering back. But he didn't know what to say anyway so he said nothing, just continued to stand there and let his grandma talk about God and praise Jesus and thank the cops for a job well done.

The car wasn't banged up at all, just smelled like beer and burnt rubber. Travis looked in the back and saw that all the groceries were still there, thinking that at least he wasn't going to have to go grocery shopping with Grandma Baxter again today.

Thirty minutes later the car was cooled down enough to drive. And even though Grandma Baxter crept home at twenty miles an hour, Travis didn't say a word about how long she was taking. He didn't want to get her started and have to hear another lecture about busted radiators and it being God's way of reminding them that they needed to slow down and smell the flowers, take their time and enjoy the life Jesus gave them.

"He died for our sins, you know," Grandma Baxter was always telling him, reminding him to be thankful for every day, shaming him into going to church every Sunday so he'd be saved. "Cause Jesus gave His life for you and the least you could do is take a few hours out of a week to praise His sacrifice." Travis rolled his eyes and held his tongue every time she started into one of her sermons.

When they pulled in the driveway, Grandma Baxter looked at her watch and exclaimed she was almost late for her show, could Travis be a dear and get the groceries? The Reverend Billy C. Reid Salvation Hour was coming on cable channel ten and Grandma Baxter never missed it. They showed it again at eight that night but the truly devout always caught the Saturday noon show when everything was happening live. Of course, Grandma Baxter always caught the two Sunday shows also because they were live and Grandma Baxter always said you had to see miracles when they actually happened or they didn't count.

Travis toted the brown grocery bags in the house two at a time, thinking to himself, *ain't no way she's going to be able to eat all this food.* He set the bags on the kitchen counter, emptying them one by one, putting them up as he did 'cause he'd been helping Grandma so long now he knew her kitchen better than her.

He put up the cheese and the ham and the bologna.  He put up the collard greens and the pinto beans and the lima beans.  He put up the eggs and the bacon and the milk.  He put up the Peanut Butter Crunch and the Funyuns and the Heineken.

*Heineken?*

Travis didn't remember getting any beer and knew Grandma Baxter didn't drink it.  She was a fundamental Baptist and didn't even believe in dancing, much less drinking.

Travis walked into the living room and said, "Hey, Grandma?"  She was glued to the Reverend Billy C. Reid preaching on TV about how the Lord giveth and the Lord taketh away and how the Lord worketh in mysterious ways.

"Shhh," Grandma Baxter said without looking away from the screen. She sat in her easy chair with a plaid shawl over her legs, the same plaid shawl she said she'd made when she was a little girl and they couldn't afford to buy blankets 'cause money didn't grow on trees.

Travis couldn't believe his grandma just shushed him.  He was practically a grown man now, having turned sixteen last month with a little peach fuzz to prove it.  He was even considering shaving for the first time and had been paying attention to the razor commercials on TV, trying to figure out if one with four blades and batteries was that much better than one with three blades and a lube strip.

Grandma Baxter got like this whenever she watched the Reverend Billy C. Reid Salvation Hour.  She rocked back and forth, her eyes fixated like she was in a trance, hanging on every word, matching her breaths to the reverend's without knowing it.

As Travis watched her, he figured out where the Heineken came from. He remembered the guys that stole Grandma Baxter's car had two grocery bags with them and guessed that when the car broke down, they took off without thinking twice, leaving their Peanut Butter Crunch and Funyuns and Heinekens behind.

Travis backed into the kitchen slowly, thinking how the Lord *did* work in mysterious ways like the Reverend Billy C. Reid said, 'cause instead of Grandma getting her car stolen, Travis ended up getting free beer and food.

He counted the bags on the counter. Six. The same number the checkout girl had packed. That meant the car-jackers had taken two of Grandma's grocery bags, thinking they had theirs. Travis laughed, figuring they probably got the bag with the Depends in it.

He repacked a grocery bag with the Heinekens and the Funyuns, took it outside and down to the root cellar where Grandma Baxter never went any more, and hid it in the far corner behind a couple jars of something that'd been there so long he couldn't tell what it was. He'd save that bag for a special Saturday night with Janice Allgood, when he wanted to do more than go to Putt-Putt and play video games.

He put up the popcorn and the Diet Pepsi and the Oreos. He put up the hamburger and the chicken thighs and the beef tips. *Who ate all this?*

Then Travis ran into something that puzzled him, made him draw his face together and try to figure out what wasn't right. It was a grocery bag with four more boxes of Peanut Butter Crunch, four *heavy* boxes. *Really heavy.*

He looked inside one, blinked, then craned his neck and tilted the box toward the light coming in from the window. He opened another box, his eyes bulging, then opened the other two boxes, still not believing his holy luck. Speechless, he slowly put it all together, figuring the whole thing out, how those guys that stole Grandma Baxter's car had left behind more than just some beer and onion rings.

Travis ran into the living room and tried to get his grandma's attention but she was still staring at the TV, hypnotized by the Reverend Billy C. Reid, his chunky face taking up most of the screen as he whined about giving to the Lord, how you get back ten times what you give. Talking about how he was raising money for America's youth, how they were coming up short on how much it was costing to build *Savior Land USA*, and if you could find it in your loving heart, send in twenty or forty or, God bless you a hundred or two, and they'd be able to construct the main attraction, the Screaming Tower of Babylon. It was going to be fifteen stories high, the tallest on the east coast, and was guaranteed to scare the demons out of you.

Travis tried to get his grandma's attention again, waving a hand in front of her like she was a plane coming in for a landing in the middle of a fog bank, waving one hand while holding a cereal box in the other, but Grandma Baxter stared right through him.

Travis returned to the kitchen for the other three boxes, held them all over Grandma Baxter's lap, and poured the contents out.

The sight and the weight of all that money finally broke his grandma from her trance. Crisp stacks of hundreds tumbled onto her thighs, covering her homemade shawl until they spilled to the floor.

Grandma Baxter's eyes bulged behind her Coke bottle glasses, like she was peering through a fish bowl, bugging out so far Travis thought he was going to have to catch them when they finally popped out.

"Lordy!" Grandma said as she picked up a few stacks. "Where'd all this money come from?"

"It was in these," Travis said, holding up the orange boxes of Cap'n Crunch, a cartoon maze on the back of all of them.

"Where'd you get those?" Grandma Baxter said, pointing at them, her face wrinkling up like her Dentu-Creme had something in it.

Travis shrugged and smiled, looked down at the boxes and said, "I don't know. They were with all the other groceries.  Nearest I can figure, them car thieves grabbed the wrong bag when they took off."

Grandma Baxter shook her head, saying, "Well, Lordy be!"  She took off her glasses and squinted real hard, bringing a stack up so close to her face Travis thought she was going to take a bite, see if it tasted as good as it looked.  Then she pulled it away, put her glasses back on and said, "What should we do?"  She paused and tilted her head.  "How much you think it is?"

Travis was thinking it was enough to get him a brand new GMC Jimmy, one with leather seats and a moonroof and running boards and a six-CD changer in the back.  Thinking it was enough to get him every kind of video game ever made and a sixty inch plasma screen to play them on. Thinking it was enough to eat sirloin tips and baked potatoes every night for the rest of his life.

Then he said, "I ain't counted it yet."  He picked up a stack, counted the hundreds in it, set it aside, and picked up another.  He had visions of Nikki Brown fawning over his new leather coat and cowboy boots, wanting him to take a picture of her with his new mobile phone, take her for a long drive in his new Jimmy, take his new boat along and go out on the lake for the day, maybe even skinny dip when it got late in the afternoon.

* * *

GRANDMA BAXTER turned back to the TV.  The Reverend Billy C. Reid had asked everyone to join him in prayer, then clasped his hands together and raised them over his head.  He shook them and looked up at the theater

233

ceiling, tilting his head so far back that everyone watching could see his nest of nose hairs curling around in there.

Travis counted while Grandma Baxter closed her eyes and the Reverend Billy C. Reid prayed, asking for forgiveness for everyone in the viewing audience and their families even if they weren't watching, praying for all the souls that needed saving, even the Muslims, begging to be given the strength to carry out His word another day, praying for the rest of the funds to finish *Savior Land USA*, saying he knew his viewers would come through, that three million wasn't all that much in the grand scheme of things. Amen.

While she was praying, Grandma Baxter's mind wandered to her car and how God would want her to get a better one with the money. Maybe a Lincoln Towncar, a new one, with heated seats and a key chain thingee so she could start it from the house on cold winter mornings. Then she thought that maybe that's what He was really telling her today with the busted radiator. She nodded her head; that's exactly what He was saying. Maybe there was enough to get Travis a car too. He was such a good boy.

Then the Reverend Billy C. Reid brought his face back to the camera, looking straight through the TV and into Grandma Baxter's inch-thick glasses, saying he had an important announcement. They'd just had a caller offer to match everything pledged in the next ten minutes. "For every dollar you give," the Reverend Billy C Reid said, "It brings us two dollars closer to our goal." He knew there were selfless people out there who wanted to save the god-fearing Christian youngsters of America from certain and eternal damnation.

"Two million! There's a little over two million in here!" Travis yelled out.

The words shook Grandma Baxter from her trance and she looked from the smiling Reverend Billy C. Reid to her smiling grandson to the stacks of money and back to the TV.  The money again and back to the TV.

*Why, what with that feller matching what everybody gives, there'd be enough left over to get two new cars, and a new fridge from Lowe's that popped ice cubes right out of the door, and even save some for Travis' college ...* She broke into a crooked grin and wondered if that Screaming Tower of Babylon was something she'd like riding on or was it too much for her?

"Funny?  You want funny?
I got funny dribbling down my leg."

*Ross Cavins*

# About the Author

**Ross Cavins** graduated with a BS in Computer Science from UNC Greensboro. He currently works as a freelance website designer and internet programmer and lives in the North Carolina Piedmont.

Two divorces and a mid-life crisis pushed him to pursue his life-long dream of writing a book. This is as close as it gets for now. His primary goal is to one day visit a bookstore and hear, "Hey, is this you?" instead of, "Hey, you gonna pay for that?"

His work has appeared in Swill Magazine, Hiss Quarterly, USA Deep South, Hack Writers, Dead Mule, and elsewhere. He's much funnier in person.

You can find him at his website: **RossCavins.com**

www.ingramcontent.com/pod-product-compliance
Lightning Source LLC
Chambersburg PA
CBHW070001120726
47909CB00003B/772